I0541567

RECYCLED

Robin Tidwell

Rocking Horse Publishing, St. Louis, Missouri

First printing, July 2013
Second printing, September 2014

Copyright © Robin Tidwell, 2013
All rights reserved.

ISBN 10: 0989568520
ISBN 13: 978-0989568524

Cover design by Shannon Yarbrough, St. Louis, Missouri
Cover photo by LeAnn Areford, St. Louis, Missouri

The characters and events in this book are fictitious.

www.RockingHorsePublishing.com

BOOKS BY ROBIN TIDWELL

REDUCED

REUSED

RECYCLED

SO YOU WROTE A BOOK: NOW WHAT?

DEDICATION

To those who loved REDUCED and REUSED, and pushed me to finish RECYCLED.

ACKNOWLEDGMENTS

I want to thank my editor, Peggy, who has consistently good suggestions, does an excellent job, and manages to entertain as well as inform while working on my book.

And of course, I'm very grateful for my family who didn't mind (much) foraging for their own dinner more than a few times during this process, living in a slightly-less-than disgustingly filthy house for several weeks, and were able to mostly communicate with me while I was lost in my characters.

Prologue

Jules followed the river as far south as she could see it. When she reached Canton, just to the north of the town itself, she came to the spot where they'd crossed less than a week ago. The muddy water of the Spoon River still churned and burbled; the banks were crumbling and soft. She sat down beneath a tree to rest in the shade, and contemplated her strategy.

Quiet, serene, and confident in her assertions to her family, Jules was now faced with the task of making some hard choices.

She could, as she'd stated to her mother, continue on to St. Louis. Mario was there, after all, and she really did want to be with him, to help him build his vision for the city, for his family. But . . .

There was David. Somewhere out West. Somewhere; that was the key. She knew where he'd been headed, but of course, there was no way to know if he'd actually gone there, or even he was still alive. Maybe . . .

Jules kept going 'round and 'round, leaning first one way and then another; which direction, which choice, where to go first.

Finally, she stood up, brushed off her jeans, and started walking. Either way, she'd be going to St. Louis. By the time she arrived, she'd have decided which course to follow, to stay or to go. Plenty of time to think.

Robin Tidwell

Chapter One

"Hallefrickinluia!" Alison clapped her hand over her mouth as the word exploded into the darkness. She was so excited she dropped her flashlight. Hastily retrieving it, she smacked it a few times before the light came on again, and shined it around the small room. She quickly climbed the ladder and ascended into the kitchen of the abandoned camper, turning off the light once again, making her way quickly back to the others.

The door flew open, and Alison was instantly covered by three weapons pointed directly at her head.

"Sorry," she said, "but you are not going to believe this!"

Guns were holstered, and Brad grabbed her by the shoulders. "You almost got shot, dammit! What's so important that you completely forgot protocol and just busted in here?"

"Chill, Brad." Alison poked him in the chest, and he immediately released her, sitting back down at the table. "I went over to my friends' old camper, the one I found yesterday. Guess what was there?"

Abby looked at her. "Guns or tequila, if I have to guess," she said drily.

Alison rolled her eyes. "If it was tequila, the bottle would be out and open and poured by now. So, no to the tequila—but the guns, yes!

"I was poking around in the camper, and I noticed a shadow on the island in the kitchen. When I looked a little closer, that's when I saw the trapdoor. I guess that explosion when we were down by the river was felt up here too, and knocked everything out of line. So I opened it, and there was a set of stairs going down. Well, really more like a ladder." She paused to take a drink of water.

"And?" prompted Brad.

"Glock, Sig Sauer, Beretta, an entire case of Taser M26Cs, and enough ammo to start a war." Alison rattled off the list. "They also had half a dozen lockers along the walls. Didn't stick around long enough to break into those."

Abby was stuffing things into her backpack. "Condition?"

Alison shrugged. "About like this place. But a little bigger." She winked at Brad. "More room for us, for sure, plus we'll be sitting on our own ammo dump."

"EJ!" Abby called her daughter from the back bedroom. "Let's go!"

Brad was the last one out, as the others scanned the darkness for light or movement. The four walked on the edge of the street, staying near the rows of campers, and within minutes arrived at their new base and got to work.

Abby and Alison went below to catalog and sort the weapons, and EJ and Brad worked on camouflaging their presence in the camper. Window shades were pulled down, any openings to the outside were covered with blankets scrounged from the cabinets and closets, and the back door was boarded up from the inside. Dawn was approaching, and they needed to be out of sight before the sun rose.

Several days later, loaded with ammo and additional weapons, the foursome moved on . . . to Chicago. Just five days' travel away, this would be their go-to place, their refuge, if things got sticky. And, of course, a place to regroup and resupply, if necessary.

They reached I-80 near midnight of the second day. The highway stretched out before them, mostly intact, smooth and dark. Ditches on either side would provide some semblance of cover, and they watched the skies constantly.

Traveling on until dawn, they made camp in a wooded area just north of Ottawa.

Brad took the first watch until noon; Abby would relieve him then for the hottest part of the day. She didn't mind. It was too hot to sleep then anyway, and after a quick nap later, she'd be ready for the long trek tonight. They still had nearly 60 miles to go to the outskirts of Chicago. She really wondered what they'd find there, and was particularly concerned, based on Alison's description, how far out the boundaries were set —and how big a reach the government had there.

She fell asleep, still thinking . . .

The sound of choppers intruded into her dreams and Abby was instantly awake, motionless, looking through the branches overhead. There it was. A flash of sunlight on metal. And the sound . . . She didn't care if she never heard them again, but that was a moot point. They didn't care about anything except their own power.

She moved cautiously over to where Brad was gazing upward.

In answer to her unspoken question, Brad said, "Four. Flying southwest."

Abby's heart skipped a beat. Surely Jules had made it to St. Louis by now. It had been six days since she'd left. Even supposing she'd laid over an extra day somewhere, she'd be close. And she'd hear them coming. Abby took a deep breath.

No sense in worrying; there wasn't a damn thing she could do about it anyway.

"Let's lay low here, maybe another day. We'll see if they come back before sunset. Otherwise . . .

Brad went to rest, and Abby took his spot under the cedar tree. It reminded her of home, what had been her home for so many years. She wished she was back there right now.

Not exactly a prodigy, Abby had worked hard in school and finished several years ahead of her classmates. She'd bummed around the Southwest for a short time and then returned to her hometown of St. Louis and had taken a "real" job. When her friend Cal approached her about a potential storm cloud breaking over the US, she'd been skeptical . . . for all of two days.

The more she'd read, the more she'd learned, the better prepared she'd become. Under Cal's direction, she stockpiled ammo, food, and weapons, and brushed up on her tracking and scouting skills. She went in on the purchase of several customized trucks for their small group, and made emergency escape plans with the others. By the time VADER was unleashed, they were all ready.

A dozen of them, friends from long ago, some close and in touch with each other, but some not seen for ten years or more, had all gathered at the old camp south of St. Louis.

The next few years had taken a toll on them all. Hiding, surviving . . . death. So many gone. She and Brad were the only ones left, and she'd almost lost him too. Almost. He was dead, then he wasn't . . . and now he was here with them, and Alison and EJ.

And Emmy. A day didn't go by that Abby didn't think of her. That terrible day, ten years ago.

Now they were on their way to Chicago . . . for what? Abby knew, but she didn't want to know, hadn't wanted to go. The children, yes, Elizabeth and Johnny. And the others who'd been taken and held prisoner. But all of this . . . this VADER, this senseless rounding up and killing and making life miserable. Always hiding, and watching. And waiting.

She broke out of her reverie at the sound of the choppers returning . . . to Chicago? Where had they been? She checked her watch. Time to wake up Alison.

Robin Tidwell

Chapter Two

Alison peered through the field glasses and tried to bring the images into focus. There it was again: movement, and a quick, bright reflection. She nudged Brad, lying next to her on the ridge, and he swung his own binoculars in the direction in which she pointed. The two of them slid backwards down the slope and quickly made their way back to the campsite.

Abby and EJ were waiting, guns ready, alert; they relaxed a bit as Brad and Alison walked into the dim light of the small fire.

"We're close enough, in the 'burbs anyway, that it could just be some random person out for a stroll," Brad said. "But I don't think so. From what we know, Chicago is even more tightly controlled than St. Louis was, and at this point . . . "

Abby nodded. "No way someone's just out wandering around. Not in the daytime. And not in this area." She gestured in a wide circle. "Every town around Chicago is deserted and nothing but rubble. We were lucky to find this place in Bolingbrook, and luckier still that whoever lived here was at least a little bit prepared."

EJ was still cataloging the ammo store they'd discovered in the basement, buried in a concrete wall that had partially collapsed during what they assumed were many flyovers in the area. Plenty of canned goods too, and even some "extras," things they hadn't run across in years, like chocolate . . . and tequila. Alison was ecstatic, and even fairly temperate, under the circumstances.

"So," said Alison, "what next? Go into the city? And start where?"

Abby was lost in thought. They waited patiently.

"I'm concerned," she finally said. "There's an awful lot of loose ammo up this way. I'm wondering how the hell all these people disappeared if they had arsenals like the one here and the one back at the campground. I think we need to be very, very careful. Something's not right."

Then it hit her. Abby's mind raced. Nothing between St. Louis and Chicago. No one around at all. No signs of life, until they were at the river. Giant explosion. Ammo dump at the campground. Same thing here. And then there was Alison and Brad's reconnaissance.

"We're poaching," she said.

Alison looked at her. Brad paused, his fork in the air. EJ spoke first.

"Someone left all this here on purpose. Someone who's coming back. Or planning on it, anyway."

"Yes," said Abby. "That. Besides, why did we end up here, of all places? I mean, we got lucky with the route we took, or we would have missed Bolingbrook entirely. But why did this house seem our best bet? For the very same reason someone else thought so too. It doesn't stand out, but it's structurally sound, as far as we can tell.

"Why this one, and not the others?"

The three adults looked around uneasily. EJ had gone back to her book, having contributed all she could at the moment. Abby was a little surprised at her daughter. She seemed to be able to switch back and forth between conversations and activities and still be paying attention to both, and quite intuitively as well.

"We need to go," said Alison. Brad nodded.

"No," Abby told them. "We need to wait. Right here. At least until dark, maybe longer. You saw someone, someone who can only be on our side. They were careless for a moment, but they'll be here.

"I'll take the first watch."

EJ went back to her lists while Alison and Brad began to load the packs. They'd wait, as Abby said, but eventually they'd all be on the move again. They made plans for a quick getaway, if necessary, and divided supplies accordingly.

By eight o'clock, darkness had fallen. They were ready, for whatever happened. Abby and Brad took positions at the front windows, Alison on the east side of the house. EJ was watching the back, under strict instructions to grab an adult if she saw anything at all.

Hours passed. And then . . . a shadow appeared to move. Then another. The silence was profound, both outside and within the walls.

Abby gave a low whistle, and the silence was broken by four distinct clicks. How many? And who? Would they rush the house, or use stealth? They waited.

The very last thing Abby or anyone else expected was a polite, but firm, knock on the front door.

She gestured for Brad to open the door while she covered him. She hoped that EJ and Alison were out of sight. She took a deep breath and released it as the door slowly opened.

A woman entered, followed by several others. Her bright blue eyes surveyed the room. Her compatriots spread out behind her as she stepped further inside. All were armed. Heavily.

"Hello, Abby," she said. "Brad. Where are the other two?"

Abby swallowed, hard. This was . . . this couldn't be . . . She blinked.

The woman gave Abby a penetrating look and then said, "Relax. We aren't going to shoot you. Probably."

Brad cleared his throat, concerned that Abby did, for once, seem speechless. "Who are you?"

"My apologies. My name is Riley. I'm part of the resistance in this area. We've been watching you ever since the river incident.

"And as long as I've tendered my regrets in regards to introductions, let me also say that I'm sorry you were caught up in that."

Brad raised an eyebrow. "You know about that?"

"Of course," said Riley. "We engineered it. Now, let's sit down and discuss the plan, civilly, if you don't mind. And if you'd invite Alison to join us, and perhaps EJ?"

Riley sat down on the rug, cross-legged, and placed her sidearm next to her. The rest of the newcomers followed suit, and Brad called to Alison. In a moment, she and EJ appeared.

Abby sat down too, warily. She was dumbfounded. This woman . . . this Riley . . . she looked like Emmy. Kind of. She sounded like Emmy. Sort of. But she wasn't. Was she?

Abby had known Emmy better than anyone. But it couldn't be Emmy. Even if she hadn't been killed, it had been ten years. She'd have come back long before now. Abby mentally shook herself and managed to concentrate on the discussion. Nominally.

"I'll start at the beginning, but I'll be brief. We don't have much time." Riley smiled. Abby's heart skipped a beat. It wasn't Emmy. She knew that. She'd keep repeating that to herself.

"Since I've been here in the Chicago area, our little group has grown from half a dozen to over 500 rebels. We've been quiet, but not invisible. We have a few people in key positions downtown, but not enough yet to stage our final strike.

"We do have connections down around St. Louis, and that's how we knew you were coming. We were hoping that, based on what we knew about you all, you'd find this particular house. And you did. You may," Riley interjected with a smile, "have been slightly put on the right track by a few casual redirects."

Brad and Alison exchanged glances. Abby was thinking furiously. Focus, she told herself. Redirects? How? She kept silent, however, as Riley went on.

"The Spoon River incident, well, I really am sorry you got caught up in that. We weren't exactly expecting the effects to be felt so far from Rockford."

"You blew the arsenal?" asked Brad incredulously.

"Well, yes," said Riley, "but relax. We got the good stuff out first. Almost everything, in fact. But we sure made the explosion look good." She gestured at one of her companions. "Sam here took care of that. She's a demolitions expert.

"Anyway, we didn't expect the Spoon River to be involved as far south as you were. Apparently, there's a fault line running down that way which opened into the underground river. Thankfully, you all made it out alive."

Abby found her voice. "So you knew we were coming, and you knew where we were as far back as the cave-in. How?"

"All in good time, Abby. Now, let me bring you up to speed here. As I said, we don't have much time. You've likely figured out that this is one of our bases and that we have quite a lot of rather useful items stored here. However, this house is just one of several scattered around Chicago's suburbs, and right now we need to be moving. Never stay in one place for too long, as I'm sure you know.

"Sam will stay here with you all while the rest of us move out. She'll guide you, and we'll talk more then, after you've arrived and settled in."

Riley looked at each of them for a long moment, and Abby last of all. Hearing no opposition to her plans, she rose, and her contingent followed her out the door, disappearing into the darkness.

Before the sun came up, they had reached the safe house in Elmhurst. The four of them shared a cubicle in the basement, remodeled for the war that seemed to be approaching more rapidly than they'd expected. Abby still didn't seem quite herself, and Brad was concerned.

"What's up, Ab? You seem okay with us being here, so what's going on?"

Abby didn't answer for a long moment.

"Did you see it, Brad? Riley. It's . . . she's not . . ." Abby waved her hands helplessly in the air. Finally, she managed to whisper, "Emmy."

Brad looked at her as though she'd gone crazy—and, given the last few years or so, it wasn't really surprising.

"She's not Emmy, Ab. She can't be. Not possible. Noah told you he saw her body, after the explosion."

"I know. But . . ."

"No 'buts,' Abby." Brad's voice grew stronger. "Emmy would have found you long ago, if she'd lived. You know that."

Brad took her by the shoulders and looked into her green eyes. "Even if they'd taken her when they came for Pops and did to her what they did to me, she'd have come back as soon as she could escape, as soon as she realized what happened. You know their brainwashing was half-assed, at best."

Brad looked over at Alison and tilted his head in EJ's direction; Alison put her arm around the girl and led her from the room. EJ glanced back her mother, worried, but went with Alison without argument. Brad turned his attention back to Abby.

"Now, look, kiddo, you have to keep it together. For EJ. For all of us. Okay?"

Abby nodded, but her mind was whirling. Yes, Noah had seen Emmy's body after the explosion, lying near Ted. He'd told her that himself. And then he dragged himself to the creek and passed out. What had really happened that day?

Brad helped her to her feet, and Abby visibly squared her shoulders. She took a deep breath. Brad started to speak, but she held up a hand.

"No. Don't say any more. I'm done; it's over. I know Riley isn't Emmy, and no 'buts' this time, okay?" She tried to smile, but couldn't quite manage it. "Really, Brad, I'm fine now. Every now and then, well, it just comes out, you know?"

Brad looked skeptical, but he went along with it and took Abby's words at face value. He'd be keeping an eye on her, though, for sure. They went out into the makeshift hallway to find Alison and EJ, who ran to her mother for a hug. Abby held her tightly for a long moment before she went in search of Riley.

She almost collided with her in the narrow corridor, and it took all of Abby's self-control to maintain her composure. She

13

held her resolve, however, and abruptly told Riley why they were there.

"The children," Abby said. "That's our priority. And afterwards, well, then we're at your disposal. But two of ours were taken, along with others, and they're here. Somewhere in Chicago."

Riley appeared only mildly surprised at this turn of events, and if she wondered why Abby hadn't mentioned it until now, she refrained from comment. "Tell me more," she said, not unkindly. "Come into my room and we'll talk."

Abby sat down gingerly on the edge of the single cot set against a wall. She was nearly back to her usual self, but still slightly agitated and quite curious. She was hoping to find some answers. Taking a deep breath, she told Riley the story of the missing children and the raid on the holding facility in St. Louis.

"So," she finished, "rumor has it that there's a place downtown where the children are being held—Elizabeth and Johnny and the others—but so far we've had no information as to its exact location or any other details. We came up here to find them and bring them out."

"But not to stop Co-opCom?"

"Yes," said Abby, resigned. "Yes, to stop them. But first, the children." She was not backing down on this. "Once they're safe, we'll do what we can. If we don't," she shrugged, "nothing else will matter anyway."

"Very true," answered Riley. "Here, let me show you something." She turned and dug through a trunk at the foot of the cot, tossing items on the bed in a random fashion. Just like Emmy used to.

Abby mentally shook herself and tried to concentrate as Riley handed her a single sheet of paper, a photograph. She looked at it questioningly.

"It's the Contemporaine, downtown. Fifteen floors, mostly glass exterior, high-priced residential. Or it was. All of the lower floors, up to the tenth, have been boarded up. We've heard about things going on there, but we haven't seen any real activity. And frankly, there have been plenty of other issues with a higher priority. Until now."

Riley pointed out the cantilevered balconies, adding, "It shouldn't be too difficult to move in close and see what's happening, even stage a rescue if that's where the kids are being held." She pulled out a city map, showing Abby the exact location on Wells Street.

Abby smiled and nearly laughed aloud. Not too difficult? Well, no, not in light of some of the things they'd accomplished the last few years or so. She studied the map.

The Contemporaine was situated due east, fewer than twenty miles from the safe house. Just past the Chicago River, right in the center of the city .

"What's in the area now?" asked Abby.

Riley shrugged. "Same things, only new and improved. Ha. The 'approved' area stretches along the lake, from Wrigleyville on the north side on down to the Stevenson Expressway. The western boundary is the river.

"We can get you across the river, and I'll loan you however many people you need."

"Fine," said Abby. "Alison and I will go in tonight and scout out the area." She took the map that Riley handed to her and scanned it, memorizing the directions as Riley spoke.

"Follow the tracks until they branch off, and take the southern route. That will point you due south just past I-94.

Keep going until you see the old Tribune building; that's where you'll cross the river, just before it, on West Grand Avenue. You don't dare go any further, not just the two of you anyway, or you'll run right into one of their biggest barracks on Canal Street.

"After that, your target is three blocks to the east. How you get there after you cross the river is up to you." Riley ran a hand through her short brown hair. "We don't have much intel from that area. We know they're working on something, something to do with VADER, but that's it. And we have no idea how heavily the east side of the river is patrolled. The entire Loop seems to be carrying on as if nothing at all had happened."

Abby looked up questioningly.

"A lot of Chicago was 'protected' from VADER, if you know what I mean," Riley explained. "More people here than anywhere else. So when the government moved its base of operations from DC, there was a lot of celebrating, a real party going on downtown. And these people, well, they thought they were entitled to the best of everything. So to keep the peace, for the few elite to stay in control, they got it."

Abby nodded. She knew. She'd seen it in St. Louis, on her first few trips into the city before it had been bombed by Colonel Barton.

Riley continued. "When it all went down here, so they tell me, there were very few families who lost anyone. I mean, sure, some groups were completely wiped out, but for the most part no one was in mourning. And the grid never went down, at least not for more than a couple days. Most weapons were turned in voluntarily, although there weren't as many as you'd think. Then again, most of these folks weren't the thinking type to begin with . . . "

"Wait a minute—you weren't here then?"

"No, Abby. I've only been in Chicago for seven years."

The two women stared at each other for a full minute.

Riley turned away first and picked up a piece of paper, handing it to Abby. "Go see Gene, three doors down from here, to your left. He'll have some equipment for you and Alison. Report back to me when you return."

The door closed behind Abby, and Riley sat down on her bunk, head in her hands, thinking . . . and remembering the day she'd arrived in Chicago.

Abby went in search of Gene, trying to make sense of her whirling thoughts. Not only did this Riley resemble Emmy or, let's face it, look a hell of a lot like her, she apparently had at least one of her habits as well: randomly tossing items from an already messy trunk onto her bed, willy-nilly. Yes, yes, Abby told herself angrily, a lot of people were slobs, and that certainly didn't prove anything.

Besides, Emmy was never the take-charge type unless she was directing an event or planning a party. No way she'd be commanding a group of rebels up here in Chicago. And anyway, where was Riley before she came here? Still more questions than answers.

Abby handed the list to Gene, and he promised to have everything ready for their departure at 1800 hours. Then she went to find Alison and Brad.

EJ was having a great time. Children were a rarity since Co-opCom took over, and about half the members of the resistance group were old enough to have grandchildren. Except they didn't. Not anymore. EJ visited and chattered more than she usually did, but she also listened and learned. She was especially entranced with Storm, a woman of indeterminate age, who was the group's healer.

Storm introduced herself to Abby at the midday meal and, after learning of Abby's upcoming mission into the city, asked if EJ could stay with her until they returned.

"Please, Mom?" EJ begged. "Storm knows all about plants and herb and things, just like in my book." She held up the worn volume. "She can teach me all kinds of things!"

"We'll talk about it, EJ," said Abby. "Now, come along, help me pack."

"But Mom, Uncle Brad will be around here too, and . . . "

"EJ, listen to your mother. That is your first lesson." Storm spoke quietly, but it had an immediate effect on the little girl, who clapped her mouth shut and rose to follow Abby.

Back in the room, Alison and Brad were filling packs and checking weapons. Abby checked her own guns, loaded up her ammo, and tried to concentrate while EJ begged again to be allowed to stay with Storm.

"Don't worry so much, Ab," Brad said. "She'll be fine, she'll learn some useful stuff, and I'll be here hanging out with Gene. We're going to go over his stock and make a list of some extras we may want to, er, acquire at some point. You know, if we happen to run across anything just lying around somewhere." He winked, and Abby relented.

"Oh, all right, EJ. Just behave yourself and stay in the house. No wandering outside, no nighttime 'missions,' okay?" Abby hugged her daughter and sent her off down the hallway. After all, EJ had survived her very birth out in the woods, no one to help except a ten-year-old Jules; she'd be fine.

Thinking of Jules, Abby wondered how she'd fared on the trip back to St. Louis. She knew, of course, that they'd likely not be hearing from her for a long time, so she put Jules out of her mind for now. This reconnaissance trip was more pressing at the moment, and she needed to focus.

It was tougher for Alison. Surely Jules had been in St. Louis for at least a few days now, even considering that she may have run into trouble. Still, a mother always worried, even if her daughter was an accomplished marksman and experienced traveler. Abby looked over at her friend. Alison showed no outward signs of concern.

Alison zipped up her pack and hoisted it onto her back, eager to get moving. She nearly collided with Riley on her way out the door, skidding to a stop. Alison looked questioningly at the rebel leader.

"What's up, Chief? Did we hit a snag?" She seemed rather disappointed.

"No," answered Riley, smiling. "We just got word from St. Louis. Your daughter arrived safely, yesterday morning."

Alison visibly relaxed and her voice wavered a bit as she asked, "Is she all right? How was her trip? Did she run into any trouble?"

Riley held up a hand to stop her. "I'm sorry," she said. "We have all we can do to keep the lines of communication open without going into a lot of extraneous and personal detail. She's arrived, she's safe and well." Riley turned to leave; then paused.

She looked at Abby and started to speak. Then she stopped, turned, and hurried down the hall and out of sight.

"What was that all about?" asked Alison.

Abby shrugged. Obviously, Brad had said nothing more to Alison about their discussion. "Let's go," she said shortly.

They walked out into the night, cautiously following Third Street until they reached East End Park. Skirting the perimeter, they ducked under the Eisenhower Expressway and made it to the rail yard within an hour and a half. So far, so good. They saw no one and heard nothing, not even a bird or a feral cat. Silence reigned, and almost total darkness.

Neither woman spoke. Each was wrapped in her own thoughts, and they'd been together too long and dealt with too much to have a need to verbalize directions or warnings. They stayed close to each other, silently walking, thinking of both the mission ahead and those they'd left behind.

By ten o'clock, they reached the Des Plaines River. Crossing wasn't an issue; the water was so low they could wade the entire span. The area beyond the river was a greenbelt, or had been. The edges were mostly sporting scrub and junk trees; further in, the trees stretched high into the blackness of the night. Still, no sounds. Abby had a brief flash of homesickness as they stopped to rest.

Dammit, she thought. Emmy. Riley. She had to stop this ridiculousness and get her act together. She shook herself mentally and finally spoke.

"Alison, I promise I'm not totally losing it."

Alison glanced at Abby. "Oh, I didn't really think you were. At least not for more than a minute. Want to talk about it?" She handed Abby a flask. "Take a drink. One won't hurt, and it'll loosen you up. I'm dying of curiosity over here!"

Abby took a deep breath. And a drink. Then one more. She grimaced. Hadn't a clue how Alison could stand this stuff. Ugh. But she did relax. A little.

"It's Riley."

Alison rolled her eyes. "I knew that much, duh."

"She reminds me of . . . Emmy. I mean, a lot. A whole lot." Abby bit her lip.

Alison sat up straighter and looked steadily at Abby. "How?"

"Her height, her build, some of her habits."

20

"I see," said Alison. "That's it?"

"Yeah. I know how it sounds. Probably thousands of people fit those categories, some or all of them, at least back when. Now, maybe a few dozen." Abby was a little annoyed with herself, once she put words to her impressions. She was starting to think she was indeed losing it, or at least suffering from some age impairment.

"Uh-huh," said Alison. "Anything else?" She watched Abby closely.

Abby shrugged. "Her eyes, mostly. The rest - coincidence, I suppose. It's just . . . uncanny."

Alison jumped to her feet and reached down to pull Abby up beside her. "Yeah, uncanny. Weird. Now, come on. Let's get going."

Abby frowned a bit, wondering why Alison was in such a hurry to end the conversation, but she knew, too, that they did have to keep moving. Still a long way to go.

They reached the Union Pacific yards around one in the morning and chose to angle to the south; they'd had no word on any activity around there. Silence still surrounded them, and darkness. Three more miles and they'd turn due south, then cross the Chicago River. If all went well.

BOOM!

BOOM!

Before the first bomb had finished echoing through the night, Abby and Alison were clambering over rails and under boxcars as fast as they could move, and as far as they could go. They stopped, huddled beside a locomotive, when they ran out of cars to hide behind.

"What the hell?" demanded Alison. "How far off was that, do you think?"

"About half a mile to the north," said Abby. "What's up there?"

"Amtrak station. Surprised no one blew it up before now," Alison smirked.

BOOM!

It sounded closer . . . and then they heard the choppers.

Chapter Three

Jules had indeed made it to St. Louis, and was just congratulating herself on doing so without running into any snags, when she was roughly grabbed from behind.

"Don't move," said a gravelly voice in her ear. His breath was about to make her gag, and she was afraid that if she did move, she'd vomit.

Her hands were bound behind her back, and she was swiftly stripped of her weapons. The man shoved her along from behind and said only, "I'm takin' you to the Boss."

Jules protested, "But - I'm a friend, I'm here to see Mario. Is he here? Is that where you're taking me?"

Her captor didn't respond.

"Hey, I'm talking to you!"

"Shut up," he said mildly, smacking her on the side of her head.

Several minutes later, she was tied to a chair in a dim room. Alone. Then she heard footsteps.

Mario opened the door. "Il mio amore!" He rushed to Jules and untied her. "So it is you! My man Bruno had no idea, and he is instructed to stop all strangers and bring them directly to me.

"I am so sorry for this!"

Jules rubbed her aching wrists. She couldn't quite decide if she wanted to yell at Mario or throw her arms around him. She decided on the latter, and he held her tight for many minutes.

"But what is this, Jules?" he finally asked. "Why are you here? Where are Abby and your mother?"

"They're all fine, Mario," said Jules, gazing up at him. "I wanted to come back - to you!"

Mario looked around the room, clearly uncomfortable. He loosened his arms from around Jules and took a step back.

"What is it, Mario? Tell me now. Is there someone else?"

"No, no," he said hastily. "Nothing like that! We are rebuilding, that is all, and I am very busy. Too busy to spend much time with you, and I am afraid that you will become bored."

Jules laughed. "How could I possibly be bored? I want to help!"

"No," Mario said firmly. "It is not safe. I would not always be with you to protect you."

Jules stared at him. "Protect me? Are you serious?"

Mario nodded stubbornly. "Yes. You are here, you are with me, it is my duty."

Jules laughed again. "Mario, this is not the 1950s. Far from it. I just walked here from Chicago, alone. Last time I was here - with you - I blew up buildings. I shot men better armed than I. I've lived without civilization and protection since I was a toddler."

"But now it's different," Mario insisted. "I would have sent for you when it was safer, when we were finished and had everything in place. Two years, three, things will be better."

"Years?" said Jules incredulously. "Years? But I want to be with you now, and besides, I'm already here. Shall I leave? Go back to Chicago?"

"Of course not," Mario said. "I cannot allow that either."

"Allow?" Jules' voice went up an octave. "I don't think you understand, Mario. There is no 'allow.' I came here to be with you, my choice, and if you don't want me here, I'll simply leave." She walked to the door and opened it. Bruno blocked her path.

She shut the door and turned around.

"Mario, my love, it seems your henchman is blocking the door. I wish to leave. Immediately."

With two long strides, Mario was at her side, taking her into his arms and kissing her passionately. Jules felt as though she were melting as she kissed him back. She forgot all about leaving, and it was some time before she remembered. She pushed him away.

"This doesn't change anything," she said breathlessly. "I'm either staying by your side, in all ways, or I'm leaving and going back to Chicago. Or, I suppose, I can keep going west." She thought of David then, but it was a fleeting thought.

"Oh, but I think it does change everything, mio caro." And he kissed her again.

Jules pushed him away. But not too far. She held his hands and looked into his eyes. "Mario. Do you really want me to sit here and wait for you, and do nothing at all?"

Mario sighed. "No, Jules, that is not what I want. But I am very worried about your safety. There are very rough men around St. Louis these days. It must be what it was like in the old days, before Co-opCom, long before VADER, even. Especially to the north of the city.

"They come here, they raid us, they leave for a time. But we never know when, and my men are spread very thinly throughout our territory."

"Are there no other women here?" asked Jules.

"Of course there are." Mario smiled. "There are men; they must have women. But these women, there are not many like you, Jules. Most of them do what their men tell them, and take care of the womanly duties."

Jules rolled her eyes and told him, in no uncertain terms, "Then I suppose that's where I must begin - teaching those women that are no such things as 'womanly duties' anymore and that their men had just better accept that!"

She stalked back to the door and opened it again. "Move it, Bruno, or I'll go right through you!"

He obliged, at Mario's nod, and Jules looked back over her shoulder. "Are you coming or what?"

Mario grinned. This was going to be interesting. And probably more fun than he'd expected. But he was still concerned about her safety, and he was just going to have to go behind her back to try to keep her in one piece. If he could.

He hurried after her, pausing to whisper something to Bruno. The big man walked down the corridor, and Mario followed Jules outside into the courtyard.

Just as she thought, Mario's people had continued to use the old Lemp Brewery as their headquarters. In spite of the destruction across most of the city, this southern section had seen quite a lot of progress in the few months since Jules had been gone. They'd stopped there for a couple days before going to Chicago, but she hadn't done any sightseeing then.

The DeMenil Mansion was standing proud; the rubble in the yard had been removed and the fencing repaired. Still, jarring as it was, the entire lot was surrounded with high rolls of barbed wire, and guards patrolled around the clock.

She turned to Mario. "You've gotten a lot done since I was here last. Very impressive."

He smiled. "I have much to show you. But first, we celebrate your arrival." Jules blushed a little. She never did like being the center of attention. "Come; it is already arranged. On the way, I will give you a quick tour."

They walked up the street to the DeMenil Mansion so Jules could get a closer look, and then came back to the brewery, circling around to the back entrance. Trash had been removed; loose boards and been fixed and other small repairs had been completed; graffiti had been scrubbed from the old brick. Even the roof had been patched.

They went inside and into a large room crowded with Mario's people. Jules looked at him questioningly. Surely there had been only a handful just weeks ago when they left for Chicago, but now there appeared to be at least fifty or more.

He led her to the head of a long conference table and raised a hand for silence. "Jules has returned to us. Some of you know her; others do not. She is with me. But I assure you, she can more than take care of herself. Bruno simply got lucky. Alla salute!" He raised his glass.

Many in the crowd were curious, but those with whom she'd served in the last year were eager to see her again and introduced her to their friends and compatriots. The celebration lasted well into the night.

Afterwards, Mario took Jules back to the DeMenil Mansion. She wasn't entirely sure at this point what to expect. He kept saying things like she was his, and she was with him, but she was a little apprehensive about all that entailed. She wasn't exactly naïve, but she was young and was completely inexperienced.

He seated her on the porch and knelt beside her. "Tomorrow, Jules, we will go to see Father Timothy, if you are willing. Many things have changed, but my religion has not.

27

And if you will do me the honor of becoming my wife, I promise to love and cherish you forever."

Jules was stunned. She wasn't sure what she'd expected, but it wasn't this. Marriage? In their situation? In this day and age? She hesitated, and Mario frowned.

"What is wrong, Jules? Do you not love me? What is it?"

Jules lowered her head, blushing just a little. Then she blurted out, "I don't know how to be married!"

"There's something you know nothing about?" Mario smiled. "I, myself, only know what I've seen from my parents and from Stefanie and Carmine, God rest their souls. But this will be a new adventure for us, for both of us."

"But Mario, I don't know anything about being married! Anything at all. Stop laughing! My mom and dad split up when I was little, and his girlfriend was a mess. They fought all the time. Grammy and Gramps were old . . ."

Mario did his best to remain serious, but he was having a hard time. Jules' outburst was so uncharacteristic, she was usually so controlled, that he was finding all of this rather amusing.

"And if we aren't married, Jules, then what's the difference?"

"Well, um . . . I don't know!" Jules threw up her hands.

"So, you'll marry me then?"

Looking like an animal in a trap, still unsure, she answered softly, "Yes."

"Jules." Mario pried open her clenched hands and held them in his. "I love you."

"I love you too," she answered, confident once again. "And where are my weapons?"

Chapter Four

Thirty minutes later, the silence had returned.

Abby and Alison scrambled from their hiding place and began jogging east. They'd wasted enough time already. Sunrise was just two hours away when they reached the Chicago River.

The bridge was an older span, rusted, and blocked to traffic, of course. No one was supposed to be on the west side at all. There were pedestrian walks on both sides, ostensibly blocked as well, but Abby could see that a determined individual could certainly cross. And they were both determined.

There were few lights burning in the buildings looming to the east. Naturally, most people were still asleep. They seemed to feel quite safe in this new city of Chicago; there were no guards, at least none visible to Abby and Alison. They hoped their luck would hold.

On the east side of the bridge, they dropped down into dry, brown shrubs near a murky, non-functioning fountain. The glass building towering above was jagged and filthy, a result of the preceding ten years or so of misguided priorities and the struggle of its former tenants.

A collapsed parking garage next door provided a place to rest for a moment and to get ready for their final push to the Contemporaine.

Riley had provided red jackets, part of the official clothing for all women registered in Chicago. Each city had its own color; one for men, one for women. These were to be worn at all times or, given warm weather, carried or attached to one's person. Bags were suspect, so Abby and Alison geared up under the jackets as best they could. They'd pass as residents, assuming no one got too close or, heaven forbid, searched them.

They left the garage and made their way up Grand, staying close to the row houses on the south side, ducking beneath windows to avoid early risers.

The sky was beginning to lighten as they reached the intersection of Franklin. One more block to go, and their target was on the corner. With a quick wave, Abby directed Alison to follow her beneath the El and around past some building that used to be Binny's or Bunny's—it was hard to tell from the demolished sign out front. They crept up the alley and stopped, checking for onlookers or any military presence. Still nothing, as it had been the entire trip. Strange.

Abby pulled out her field glasses and scanned upward. Just as Riley had said, the windows on the lower floors were boarded. Alison nudged her and pointed up. Ah, the place was wired too. Good to know. It was the stuff one couldn't see that was usually the problem, and the razor wire and spikes were very visible from the fifth floor to the fourteenth.

The lower floors had once been retail space. Rumor had it that now it was used for "offices," Co-OpCom's term for special interrogation rooms, presumably so that any screams emanating from the walls could be heard that much better by passersby. Yet another way to keep the citizenry in line with the government programs.

The children were being held in the condo section, the residential tower connected to and just behind the lower floors. They were separated by age and gender, by floor, and were mostly left to their own devices when they weren't being subjected to further testing.

Co-OpCom was still trying, more than ten years later, to perfect VADER.

Abby shuddered to even think of it.

Suddenly, a loud, blaring siren went off. Abby and Alison nearly dropped their equipment as they flattened themselves against a wall. Binny's or Bunny's. They clapped their hands over their ears; the cacophony went on and on . . .

It stopped. Blessed silence. For a moment.

Lights came on all across the city, and the everyday sounds of any city, before, rose to greet the day. The sun was barely peeking over Lake Michigan, and its tendrils began to weave throughout the streets.

The two women looked at each other. "That's one hell of an alarm clock," said Alison.

They walked back to Franklin and turned left, joining the crowd who were purposefully and in near silence heading to work. Abby sarcastically thought that yes, the new regime had certainly given people what they wanted. In spite of Riley's claim that not much had changed for those in power, it was clear that those who were on the bottom rungs were safe, but completely ruled with the proverbial iron fist. No one made eye contact; all were silent.

Abby and Alison carefully emulated those around them as they reached the intersection of Hubbard. Turning east, the two fell in with a slightly different group. Some were gazing about; most had blank faces and resigned expressions. They crossed beneath the nonfunctioning El and turned onto Wells.

This route would take them past the front entrance of the Contemporaine.

Except that it didn't. When they reached the corner of Illinois and Wells, just past the former Human Rights Watch offices, a thick concrete barrier topped with barbed wire blocked the path. They realized, too, that they were alone. The people around them had disappeared, obviously having reached their destinations, and Abby and Alison stopped, wondering exactly where to go next. And, too, wondering why the entrance to the Contemporaine was so forbiddingly inaccessible, while the rear of the building was wide open.

They ducked into a recessed area at the front of the abandoned Metropolitan Bank. Alison snickered at the sign on the shuttered business next door: "Psychic Readings."

"Now what?" she asked.

"Backtrack," said Abby, "and go around the next block."

"Okay," Alison said dubiously. "But, um, have you forgotten that we're the only ones on the street? We're gonna be really easy to spot out here."

"All right. Let's shoot down this alley and go back to Franklin. We can go north a block and circle back to the other side." Abby checked her .357 and left her holster unsnapped. "Come on."

The alley was narrow and dim, cluttered with boxes and assorted junk. Obviously, trash pick-up wasn't high on Co-opCom's list of priorities. They made their way back to Binny's or Bunny's and paused to regroup.

BOOM!

"Shit!" said Alison. "Don't they ever quit? Is there a tracker on us or something?"

BOOM!

"This way!" Alison shouted, grabbing Abby's arm and pulling her towards the west, to the river. Abby didn't resist, because they seemed to be going in the opposite direction from the horrific bomb. And besides, Alison had lived here for a time and maybe actually knew where she was going.

Oddly, no people appeared outside to see what was happening. Maybe they knew, thought Abby. Maybe they didn't want to know.

BOOM!

They reached Orleans Street and turned south, still running, still alone; turning west again, down Illinois to Kingsbury. Alison stopped short, and Abby smacked into her.

"Just a sec," Alison gasped, breathing heavily. "It's around here somewhere."

"What is?" asked Abby. She'd brought her own breathing under control and appeared calm and controlled, although she was ready to run again, if need be.

"Here!" shouted Alison, grabbing on to Abby again and yanking her along as they rushed into a huge, cavernous building, surprisingly intact except for the piles of glass and jagged edges of the mostly-glass walls. It took both of them to shove open a fire door, and they ran down the concrete stairs. Alison stopped and pulled out a flashlight, shining it in all directions before taking off again, pulling Abby behind her.

There was a door marked "Authorized Personnel Only," which, of course, didn't stop them. They could still hear the bombs falling, and even muted, the sound was closer. Alison picked up a crowbar that a careless worker had conveniently left behind and pried open the door. They both slipped inside, and Abby yanked the door shut.

"Where in hell are we?" she asked.

"Subway," Alison told her.

This was not the best news, Abby mused. Blown to bits or buried alive? Not much of a choice. "Which way do we go?"

"Go?" asked Alison. "I wasn't planning on going anywhere, just getting underground and out of sight. Anyway, most of these tunnels were blocked off when they stopped using them. I figured we'd sit tight and wait until the bombs stopped.

"Besides, I'm worn out. All this cloak-and-dagger stuff is tiring." She sat down, leaning against a cold concrete wall, and stretched out her legs.

BOOM!

The tunnel shook. Bits of rock fell all around them.

Alison jumped to her feet. "Never mind. Sheesh, let's go!"

"Yes," Abby said patiently, again, "but which way?"

"Hell, I don't know! Everything is backwards down here. Or upside down. Or something. Um . . . " Alison looked around wildly. "That way!" She pointed.

Abby gave her a look. "South?"

"Yeah. Sure. South. Let's go!"

BOOM!

A large chunk of concrete fell, blocking their intended path. "Damn," said Abby. "Not south. Come on!" She grabbed Alison and took off in the opposite direction. They rounded a corner at full speed and crashed into a wall, slamming into each other before hitting the floor. Hard.

"Crap," said Abby. "Alison, you okay?" She fumbled for the flashlight and shined it around.

"Yes, yes, peachy," grumbled Alison, rubbing her forehead. "If you weren't so darned skinny, I could have had a softer landing.

"Hey, what's that?" She grabbed the light from Abby and swung it to the left. Another door.

Abby shrugged. "May as well."

The two women began pushing and pulling, trying to get a purchase on the heavy door that looked as though it hadn't been opened in decades, if ever.

At last it broke free with a loud, piercing screech. Solid darkness greeted them, and stairs. Stairs that descended into more blackness.

Abby looked at Alison. "What the heck is below a subway?"

"Beats me." Alison shrugged.

BOOM!

"Doesn't matter. It's gotta be better than this!"

Robin Tidwell

Chapter Five

Riley was pacing back and forth; not that it was very satisfying, really, since her cubicle was only ten feet square and held her cot and a trunk, as well as a table and chair. She was second-guessing her decision to send Abby and Alison into the city with no backup, and little knowledge. On the other hand, she probably couldn't have stopped them.

Back and forth.

There was a knock at the door. "Come in!" she barked.

Brad stuck his head in the door. "Is this a bad time?"

"It's not ever usually a good time. Come on in." Riley studied Brad's face surreptitiously as she waved him to have a seat. Hmmm.

"I take it you haven't heard from them?"

"No, and I didn't expect to. Either they'll come back, or they won't." Riley shrugged.

What a cold-hearted . . . Brad was convinced that Abby was wrong about Riley; Emmy could never be this emotionless. He rose to leave, holding his anger in check. "I assume you'll let me know any news?"

"Of course," said Riley.

Brad moved to the door, paused, then slammed it shut behind him.

Interesting, he thought, striding down the hallway in search of EJ. He'd barely noticed Riley's clenched fists during their brief interchange, but it occurred to him as he left the room that perhaps she wasn't quite as detached as she let on. They could all hear the bombs falling in the city. They knew what it meant, even if no intel had yet come in regarding cause or specific location.

He shook his head. He still thought Abby was wrong.

Riley went back to her pacing. Back and forth. She took a few deep breaths, letting them out slowly. It didn't help.

BOOM!

Okay, that one sounded closer. Much closer. She wondered if they should evac sooner than planned, but until Abby and Alison returned, she wanted to stay right here. Just in case.

Back and forth. Thinking. Remembering.

She'd heard the bombs before, of course. All through her brief time in St. Louis, her tenure in DC, and now here, in Chicago. Even when she was on the other side, at least by all outward appearances. At first, the heart-stopping noise and sickening sounds of impact had induced nightmares - nightmares during the day, even, made worse by the drugs.

Then, after a while, she became inured to the sounds, the thoughts of devastation and death. She schooled herself to become numb, to be stoic and blank, to be compliant. On the outside.

During her imprisonment, her captivity, she was forced to do things she'd never imagined, things she could barely face now without breaking down. So she didn't think of them. Often. Sometimes, when she was alone, they'd surface unexpectedly. Usually she could ignore those thoughts, but occasionally she welcomed them. Sometimes she needed to remember. And to remember her goal.

To go home. Somehow. Someday.

Back home to . . .

Another knock at the door interrupted this last wish, this hope.

It was Sam.

"Hey, Riley, we found the targets. Come on out to the conference room. Everyone's on their way." The door rattled as she closed it and disappeared.

Riley shook off her mental cobwebs to focus on the task at hand. She had to be strong; she had to be ready. Just like . . . Stop, she commanded herself. Not now. Maybe not ever.

Squaring her shoulders, she went to meet with her people.

"All right," snapped Riley. "How bad is it?"

"They started at Wrigley . . ." Stunned silence greeted Sam's announcement. Even though baseball hadn't been played in more than a decade, Wrigley Field was an institution, an abode of misplaced hope each season.

Sam cleared her throat. "And, um, they went south. Looks like they're moving everyone that direction, herding them in, so to speak."

"What else did they hit?" asked Riley.

"All of the churches, DePaul, Old Town, and Lincoln Park. And the homes. The entire area. They stopped just south of Loyola."

"They're moving in," said Tom, "circling the wagons."

"Have we heard from our cells in that area?" Riley demanded. "Or anywhere else?"

"Too early for anyone outside the Chicago area to report," said Sam. "Lee, what have you got from the groups up north?"

Lee cleared her throat and glanced around the room before speaking. "It's not good," she said. "We lost two cells entirely; wiped out. That would be Jim's and Evan's."

"Tom?" asked Riley. "What updates on VADER?"

"First, let me recap what we know, or have known. It's an airborne virus, unintentionally so. It kills within minutes by bursting blood vessels, starting with capillaries and progressing to major arteries. Sometimes the bodies simply evaporate. And some people are immune.

"As a researcher, I can tell you that this is something never seen before its release, and I damn certain never want to again. We simply have to survive until we can find ground zero and eliminate all traces. You know that Co-opCom has been experimenting, trying to find an antidote. At this point, it's rather, um, pointless. Those who have been affected are long dead, and no new cases have cropped up.

"But it seems as though Co-opCom has, er, lost the formula and its accompanying samples. So, as government is wont to do, they are attempting to duplicate VADER."

Incredulous shouts greeted this last statement, as Tom held up a hand for silence.

"Yes, duplicate. They think that they can tweak it just a bit and have a more accurate effect. One would imagine that if they're successful, they would create the antidote as well, but we can't be certain."

"Damn right about that," said Sam, bitterly. She'd lost her entire family within two hours, while she sat by helplessly, watching. An eight-year-old was no match against VADER.

The room broke out in pockets of anger and grief. Wisely, Riley let them continue for a few moments before clapping her hands to get their attention. This was a war, and she wouldn't let them forget it. There would be time later, someday, to mourn. Not now.

"All right. First, Lee, take Jake and go assess whatever's left up in the Lincoln Park area. See what you can find out about our two groups up there.

"Tom, you and Storm will hold down the fort here. Sam, you'll stay, too, and handle communications. Be ready for more people to show up, injured or not.

"Brad, you're coming with me. Brad!" Riley grabbed his shoulder when he didn't respond. He'd been paying attention, sure, but was fascinated with the way Riley seemed so in control, so in charge; yet, he saw something else . . .

He jumped up when she yelled at him, though, grinning sheepishly. "Yeah, okay, I got it. Let's move!" He was relieved to see EJ with Storm, and he stopped to hug her and tell her goodbye. When he began dragging out instructions to her and to Storm, reluctant to leave her after Abby's initial concern, EJ laughed.

"Uncle Brad, I'm okay. I'm here with Storm. She'll watch over me. Go find Mom, okay?" Only at this last could he see that EJ was indeed still such a little girl, too little to lose her mom, so he hugged her extra tightly one more time and turned to leave.

"We're going after Abby and Alison, right?" asked Brad, jogging to keep up with Riley. "I mean, you never actually said . . ."

"Yes," Riley said briefly.

They were moving along the tracks, following the same route that Abby and Alison had taken the night before. It took them much less time than the others to reach the river crossing at Grand Avenue, in spite of ducking behind buildings and piles of assorted rubble.

They stopped just east of the bridge. Riley pulled out her binocs and zeroed in on the unusual building several blocks from where they stood. The rising sun showed the jagged remains of the Contemporaine.

"So it's true," said Riley. "They did go all the way down to the river. If those kids were being held in that building, they either moved them, or . . . " She didn't have to continue. Brad got it, loud and clear. Now they had to find Abby and Alison.

If they were still alive.

They had no radio; no communication whatsoever. Deep in enemy territory. And so many questions: Where were they when the bombing began? And which direction did they go?

Riley sat down and leaned against a crumbling wall. Which way? Her mind raced in circles. Stop it, she told herself. Just think. Focus.

Brad watched her closely.

After several minutes, Riley stood up. She gestured to Brad, and they made their way across the bridge, into the city. The sun was rising higher, displaying a hideous scene.

Bodies. So many bodies. All those workers, all the people who'd once lived and worked here. Presumably, Co-OpCom had relocated those it deemed necessary to the workings of the government, but one couldn't really be sure.

They walked east, then south. It was eerily still and quiet. No movement, no sound. Nothing but dead bodies. Occasionally, they stopped to check movement, but it was always only a fluttering piece of paper or some loose clothing blowing in the slight breeze. No one appeared to have survived.

All the way to the bend in the Chicago River, Brad and Riley saw no one. Only death and destruction.

Back at the bridge on Grand, they stopped. Riley slid to the ground, head in her hands. This time, Brad sat next to her.

"Emmy."

Riley didn't move.

Brad put his hand on her shoulder. "Emmy."

Riley began to shake, and then sob. Brad put his arms around her and held her tight. They sat there for a long time.

At last, wiping his own eyes, probably from all the smoke, he thought, Brad lifted her chin and looked into Emmy's eyes. Yes. Abby had been right all along.

"How did you know?" she asked.

"Abby saw it the first day we met you." God, had it just been three days? Something like that. "She thought she was going crazy when she told me. I kind of blew her off, told her how impossible it was, but she was really having a hard time with it."

Emmy smiled, just a little. It disappeared so fast that Brad wasn't sure it was even there in the first place.

"Tell me what happened, Emmy. Why didn't you come back? And why . . . "

"Why do I look so different? It's a long story, Brad. I'm sure we'll have time to talk, eventually. Besides, I have a few questions for you. Last I heard, you were dead too."

"Yeah, well . . . long story," said Brad. "All right. You sent them to the Contemporaine, Grand and Wells. That's over there," he pointed, "and they came this same way, right? Across the bridge?"

"Yes," said Emmy. "Those were the directions."

"They likely followed your route, then, since Abby isn't familiar with Chicago, and when Alison was here she was stationed downtown, south of here and near the lake. And she came here after Co-OpCom took over, so there wasn't a lot of travel in this part of the city. Looks like all workers housed over here, none of the big shots.

"When did the first reports come in?"

Emmy thought for a minute. "Sam let me know right away when the first ones fell, around 0700 hours. It got bad really quickly. Abby and Alison were probably close by, a couple blocks over from here, I'm guessing."

"Right," said Brad. "Since it was coming from the north, they'd go south or west, and try to go underground. Well, not literally."

"Wait!" Emmy held up her hand. "Yes, underground, literally! Come on!" She began to move south along the river, cautiously, but quickly, picking her route carefully, and watching the skies.

Brad followed. Both drew their sidearms.

Chapter Six

The stairs went down and down, lower and lower. By Abby's count, there must have been six flights; that meant at least three stories below the Chicago subway. She'd never been claustrophobic before, but was leaning in that direction when they came to yet another door.

"Hey," said Alison, "where's the table with the potion?"

"What?" asked Abby. Her expression clearly said that Alison had lost her mind. Again.

"You know, Alice in Wonderland. Drink me."

Before Abby could respond, the door swung open and a disembodied voice spoke.

"Keep your hands where I can see them. Identify yourselves."

They complied immediately and were taken on a meandering path, nearly blind in the penetrating blackness. Their guide seemed to have extraordinary vision or perhaps was just completely familiar with the maze of tunnels. They walked for a good thirty minutes, best Abby could tell.

At last they came to a stop. Another door. Abby thought maybe Alison had been close to the mark; surely this was Wonderland, or at least a rather grim version. They were thrust through the sudden opening of the door and left alone.

Inside the room, they could hear the quiet whir of a generator and could see only within a small circle of light provided by a single blub. There were two chairs and table, the only furniture. They'd heard the snap of a lock as they'd stumbled inside, so there was only one thing left to do. They sat.

Alison pulled off her boots, rubbing her feet. Abby checked her weapons, which, surprisingly, were still in her possession. They were silent for a long time, and then both spoke at once.

"Why do you think - "

"Who are - "

"You first," said Alison.

"Who are these people? And why not disarm us?" Abby tugged on her braid, trying to think. She was pretty sure that being this far below ground was affecting her brain.

"I'm guessing," said Alison, "and only guessing, that they used to live here in the city and went, literally, underground when it all went down. As for the disarming, I got nothing. If they realized we were against Co-opCom, why stick us in here? And if they think we're with the government, why not shoot us? I would have."

Abby nodded. "So we wait."

They didn't wait long. Within minutes, two men entered the room, along with a young boy who remained guarding the door while the other two moved swiftly toward the table.

"Identify yourselves," demanded the older man. "And tell us which side you're on."

"Well, we're certainly not on the side of the government," snapped Alison, in response to his question.

Abby rolled her eyes. Way to be subtle, Ali.

"Can you prove it?" asked the younger man. He looked to be about twenty or so. It was hard to tell in the dim light, but his belligerence upon just having met them seemed to fit that age group.

"Why, yes, sonny boy. Of course, we can prove it. Just call up Co-opCom and they'll tell you all you want to know." Alison was in her best sarcastic form and she was getting more and more aggravated with this punk. "I'm sure they'll even give up all their best-kept secrets and tell you exactly why they're bombing the crap out of Chicago."

"Oh, we know why they're doing that," interjected the older man. "They're herding us in like sheep; the destruction is just a bonus.

"Jerome, settle down. No one from Co-opCom is going to send anyone into an abandoned subway. Besides, I'm sure this little lady here is gonna jump up in a second and use that knife of hers on your face, or somewhere more important, if you don't mind your manners."

Abby frowned at the "little lady" remark, but she let it pass, settling instead on giving Jerome a look that could freeze water. She turned her attention back to the other man.

"I'm Abby," she said. "And this is Alison. And no, we're not with the government. Never have been."

"Well," Alison began, "there was this one time - "

"Shut up, Ali," said Abby, mildly. "Now, we have a few questions of our own."

"Go ahead," said the man. "I'm Larry, by the way. You already know who Jerome is, and that youngster over by the door is Hawk. Don't know who his folks were, and he picked the name himself. You can thank him for still having all your weapons. He follows directions real well, but he isn't much on taking initiative."

47

Abby nodded in Hawk's direction; the boy blushed and smiled. "So we know your names. Why are you down here? And where is 'here,' exactly?"

"Well," said Larry, "we've been living down here for quite a while, ever since the first wave of bombs fell. Some of us, immune to that VADER thing, just congregated in the subway when things went to hell. We started moving some stuff down here, got a little organized eventually. And then they started rounding up survivors.

"Some of our people went back up topside, believed the promises and such. A handful of us moved lower, down to these here tunnels."

Jerome had stopped pouting, even though he still looked a little scared of Abby and her knife. "Yeah, the tunnels are pretty cool and all, if you're into history and stuff. They've been here since forever; the big, old department stores used to haul their stuff through here. That way, they didn't clog up the streets and, you know, run over people and stuff."

"I see," said Abby, trying to hide a smile. "So why didn't you disarm us? I mean, I heard what you said, but surely you'd tell Hawk to do that if he came across any strangers. I know he's young, but he's not exactly small, and I'm thinking he could easily have handled of both us, considering he took us by surprise."

"Well," Larry drawled, "we didn't really think you were down here to do us any harm. Now, Jerome here, he's just itching for a fight. Besides, he and I, we're protected." At this, he let out a low, long whistle, and the door opened.

Twenty more people crowded into the room, armed to the teeth.

"Wow," said Alison, eyeing the array of Uzis, AK-47s, and other assorted guns. "You really are protected." She glanced at Abby.

"Kenny," called Larry. "Come tell us what you know."

A young man stepped forward and nodded at Larry. "Yes, sir. The bombing has stopped. A lot of dead up top, and most of the buildings are gone north of the river as far as we can see."

"The children?" Larry asked. "They were removed safely?"

Before Kenny could answer, Abby interrupted. "Children? At the Contemporaine?"

"What do you know about that, Abby?" Larry frowned. "That was a top-secret operation. Several of our best fighters died during the rescue." The crowd seemed to move closer to the two women. Angry murmurs were rising.

"We know nothing at all about a rescue attempt," declared Abby. "Our concern is the children being held there by Co-OpCom. In fact, that was our sole purpose in coming to Chicago." She silently willed Alison to not elaborate on that.

"What's your interest in these children?"

The crowd moved in even closer.

"Two of them are ours. Elizabeth and Johnny. They were taken . . . near St. Louis." A wave of sympathy rolled through the room, and the armed tunnel-dwellers seemed to relax.

"Then come," said Larry. "We will take you to them."

Astonished and hopeful, Abby and Alison rose and followed; the others fell in behind them.

They walked for a long time. No sun, no stars, no idea of time or place or direction. Still, they could hear the river. Whether it was to the left or the right or above or below, they had no idea.

An hour later, Larry stopped and turned to Abby.

"What you see here may be shocking. Please try not to react. These children have been through a lot, especially lately."

Abby nodded.

"The rest of you," Larry continued, "may disperse. I'll be perfectly fine here with Abby and Alison and Jerome." The crowd melted away, disappearing down dark tunnels off the main route or entering other rooms to either side. They could hear doors closing softly, until they were alone with the two urbanites.

"Come. Let's visit the children."

The door opened. What Abby saw nearly broke her heart . . . and she'd thought it way past the breaking stage many years ago. She stopped so suddenly that Alison almost ran into her.

The dimly lit room was temporary quarters for nearly three dozen kids, ranging in age from about four years to sixteen or so. Some were missing limbs; some lay on pallets, moaning softly. One girl appeared to be speaking quietly to the walls while standing in a corner. Two boys were arguing, and it looked as though they'd soon come to blows.

Larry moved swiftly to the pair, separating them, and motioning to one of two women who seemed to be caregivers. She hastily came to his assistance, and the quarrel ceased.

And then they saw Elizabeth. She was sitting in a chair, head lowered, hands folded in her lap.

Abby went to her and knelt beside the chair.

"Elizabeth, it's Abby."

Slowly, the girl raised her head. She stared at Abby with blank eyes, and then dropped her chin to her chest.

Larry spoke. "She doesn't appear to know you, although you seem to have correctly guessed the name of at least one of the children we rescued. I'm afraid we'll have to leave the room now.

"Jerome! Escort these . . . ladies to the interrogation room. Bruce and Hawk are waiting outside the door. Relieve them of their weapons and restrain them."

"The hell?" said Alison, silent until this moment. "We aren't going anywhere!" She backed up a step and reached for her Ruger. Larry drew his own weapon as fast as an Old West gunslinger and covered her. The two stood there, facing off, for long seconds.

"Stop!" shouted Abby. Turning her attention back to the girl, even as she was being physically lifted to her feet by Jerome, she pleaded, "Elizabeth, look at me, tell them!"

Elizabeth didn't move, didn't utter a sound.

Abby fought and twisted and kicked, managing to reach her knife. As she pulled it and went for Jerome's throat, all bets were off. She heard the sharp report of a gun, and then screams. Jerome dropped her to the hard floor as he dived for cover. The children huddled in a corner, with their caretakers protecting them as best they could. Abby came to her feet with the knife in one hand and her .357 in the other.

Alison held the smoking gun, pointed directly at Larry's head. Oh, he was fine, albeit cowering on the floor, hands over his ears. Probably peed his pants. Alison grinned. Of course, she did.

"All right," said Abby. "I think we've had enough of your hospitality. We're taking Elizabeth and we're leaving. Now, do you have a boy here named Johnny? I don't see him, but I wouldn't put it past you to have him locked away somewhere else."

Larry raised his head. "No, ma'am, we don't have no boy named Johnny. Elizabeth asked for him over and over when we brought her here, but we couldn't find him at all. That's when she got all quiet-like."

"Fine, then. I suppose I have to take your word for it. Alison, get Elizabeth, and let's go. Larry's going to stay here with the kids, and Jerome's coming with us."

The two women had calmed the children and now came to help Larry off the floor and over to a chair.

Alison gave Larry a disgusted look. "Larry, dude, you all really need to work on your defensive skills. Always, always expect "the little lady" to pull the trigger. And in the future, you might want to first disarm anyone who finds his way down here before you start playing your little games."

Abby stopped at the door, gun still pressed into Jerome's back. "What about the rest of the kids?"

"You're right, Ab. We should take them all back to . . . back with us. Hard telling what's going to happen to them here."

"Oh, no, ma'am," spoke up one of the women. "We'll take good care of these kids, don't you worry none. Me and Jeanine here, we're good with kids. We used to be nurses before all this nonsense started."

The other one, presumably Jeanine, added, "You don't pay Larry no mind. We never had no visitors down here before, not even the government. He just did what he thought best. Go on now. You got what you came for. Take care of that little girl, and be safe.

"Jerome, you make damn sure you tell those others outside the door to let these people leave. No funny business, you hear?"

Jerome mumbled something that sounded like assent and walked through the door when Abby poked him again with the gun barrel. Alison and Elizabeth followed; the latter still silent, but compliant.

They came back outside, into the noonday sun, near the Chicago River but many blocks farther north than where they'd gone underground. Jerome hastily left them, rubbing his back and throwing a fearful look over his shoulder.

"Well," said Alison, "glad that's over." She stuck her gun back in her shoulder rig and stretched her aching muscles. "A little tense back there."

The three of them sat down to rest, Elizabeth between the two women, and surveyed the landscape. The bright, sunny day underscored the utter destruction all around them.

And then Elizabeth spoke.

"Abby, is it really you?"

She turned to Abby, and her eyes opened wide as a single tear ran down her cheek.

Robin Tidwell

Chapter Seven

Brad and Emmy continued south, slowly, carefully. It was full daylight by now, but still no people, no sounds. No choppers. Not yet.

When they reached Kinzie Street, Emmy pointed to the old Merchandise Mart. They shoved open a side door and went into the dark, cavernous building.

Marble columns leaned precipitously, and the terrazzo tile was gouged and darkened with age and misuse and neglect. Trash littered the floor.

Looking around at the yellowing posters gracefully peeling off the walls, Brad cracked, "I think my invitation got lost in the mail." He immediately regretted speaking aloud as the sound echoed for what seemed like minutes. "Okay, then," he whispered. "Sheesh, this place is creepy! Why, exactly, are we here?"

"Follow me," Emmy whispered back. She passed the elevator banks and opened the door to a stairwell.

They went down.

It took several minutes to jimmy the old steel door at the bottom of the stairs. It didn't help that a large portion of the building, all four-million-plus square feet of it, had been hit earlier that day; even the undamaged portions had been knocked askew. Brad kept looking up, as though the entire thing was going to come crashing down, burying them alive.

"There," said Emmy. "We're in the subway. Or part of it. A maintenance station."

"How'd you know this was even here?"

"I didn't. Gene told me about it once. He talked and talked about the old days and the Merch Mart. He used to work down here, after he got out of the service.

"Anyway, we just follow this corridor along the river, turn right, and keep going north."

"That's all, huh?" said Brad.

"Sure," said Emmy. "We're bound to run into them."

"If they're here," Brad reminded her.

They started walking, in silence.

An hour later, they ran into a dead end. The tunnel was filled with rubble, top to bottom. Emmy slumped to the floor. She bit her lip and looked up at Brad.

"Now what?"

"We'll have to backtrack, go topside as soon as we can. At least we can look around and maybe see . . . something. Or someone. I've had enough of this underground stuff. Sheesh. Creeps me out." Brad rubbed his forehead and tried to loosen the muscles in his shoulders.

They turned around and walked until they found a door, partially opened. The stairs beyond went just one way. Down.

"I take it you want to skip this and see what's behind Door Number Two?" asked Emmy, with a small smile. Being down here didn't bother her at all.

"Yes. Let's keep going." Brad was starting to sweat, and it wasn't because they were overexerting themselves. He tried to control his breathing, but he knew Emmy could hear him.

They'd been below the city in the warm, musty tunnels for nearly three hours now, and that was about his limit.

They surfaced at Grand Avenue, right back where they'd started. And still no sign of Abby and Alison. Both wanted to keep looking; both knew that it was futile. If they were still alive, they'd try to get back to the safe house in Elmhurst.

Which is where Brad and Emmy needed to go, too.

They climbed over a pile of rock and went into a nearby parking garage that was only partially collapsed. Shedding their packs, lining up their weapons neatly, they flipped a coin to see who would take first watch. They both needed sleep, but Emmy was pleased to see that she'd "lost." She was too keyed up to close her eyes anyway.

Brad stretched out and was snoring lightly within minutes. Emmy hugged her knees to her chest, staring out at the light beyond, reflecting off the river.

She remembered that day, of course. The day that the bombs came home, home to the camp. The day Cal lost her mind altogether and shot herself, and Pops had had a heart attack. She remembered shouting to Abby to run, to take Juliet, to be safe.

And then, nothing.

Nothing until she heard the choppers again. Except this time there was only one; one to take her and Pops away. She'd turned her head to look out and saw the remains of the old infirmary. She'd seen the bodies. Ted. Noah. That was all. Then they were gone.

They'd taken her first to St. Louis. Kept her in a small room, hooked to IVs; so many machines beeping and clicking. She had no idea how long she'd stayed there. But she could hear the bombing, even in her sleep.

When she was deemed well enough, healed physically, they moved her to DC. That's when it started.

Emmy checked her watch. Time to wake up Brad. She'd sleep an hour or so; then they'd head back. She knew there was nothing else they could do.

***

Abby and Alison were only about 100 yards north of where they'd initially crossed the Chicago River on their way into the city. The Tribune building, directly west of their current location, had sustained some damage, but most of the buildings around it and continuing west appeared to be much as they had been earlier that morning.

The bridges, however, had all but disappeared. All of them.

"This way," said Alison decisively. "The river at Ohio Street is pretty shallow. Gross, but shallow. We can climb, and if we fall in, we'll just get a little wet. And smelly."

It took several minutes to rouse Elizabeth from the catatonic state into which she'd relapsed shortly after speaking Abby's name. They literally had to guide her, one on each side, taking her arms, and they moved very slowly.

When they reached what had once been a large, beautiful condo building on Erie Street, they stopped and moved into the shade of the collapsed walls. In spite of her blank stare, Elizabeth was compliant and did as she was told, albeit very slowly, as though she were moving through molasses.

They decided to wait until dark, still a good six hours away.

***

Emmy awoke to Brad's shout, on high alert, reaching for her Sig. She stopped when she saw his face.

Brad held up a battered flask. "It's Alison's! They must have been right here at some point!"

"Yes," she said, "but before or after the blasts?"

"Oh," said Brad. "Yeah. Right. But they were here." He turned and started walking. "Let's go."

Emmy scrambled to grab her gear and catch up. She knew Brad and Alison were together; she probably should have been more sensitive. She used to be. Before.

"Brad, wait!"

"What? I just want to get back, see if they're there." And then go kick some ass, he thought, remembering all the death he'd seen and experienced. He'd had enough of Co-OpCom, even though sometimes . . . sometimes he could almost put it all out of his mind. One thing at a time. Live in the here and now. But with Alison missing. Or dead, more likely; now it was different.

They arrived at the house in Elmhurst just after midnight.

"Brad, stop. We need to talk." Emmy bit her lip. "No one here knows who I am. Or who I used to be. To them, I'm Riley. I need to keep it that way."

"I understand," said Brad, "but what about Abby?"

"I don't know yet," Emmy said with a sigh.

They went inside as Sam and the others crowded around, waiting for news. Downstairs, in the conference room, Riley asked for reports from each of them. It was obvious that Abby and Alison were still missing. EJ sat next to Brad, holding his hand tightly.

"Jake and I went north and east, as directed," said Lee. "We have confirmation that Jim, Evan, and both cells are . . . gone. We also checked on Brenda's group. They're okay. They were farther to the west, as they'd moved just two days ago, based on rumors that Co-OpCom was starting some demolition again." She frowned. "We have yet to determine the source of those rumors."

"I see," said Riley. All traces of Emmy had disappeared as her face hardened. "Gene, get on that, will you?" At Brad's questioning look, she explained, "Black Ops. Gene's the best."

"EJ and have prepared for any injured," said Storm gently. "But so far, there have been none."

"What about our people on the south side? Any word?" asked Riley.

"Nothing yet," Sam told her. "It's still early."

"Tom, you'll take over on guard, along with Sam. Keep an eye out for Abby and Alison. Storm, they may be in need of your services." Riley glanced at EJ. "I'm beat. I'm going to get cleaned up and catch some sleep. Keep me posted." Riley left the room.

Brad took EJ to their assigned room and helped the little girl get ready for bed. He wanted her close by tonight, and she didn't argue. Storm was busy anyway, or could be later, and if Abby and Alison showed up at all, he didn't want EJ on the front lines. Just in case.

***

With Alison and Elizabeth sleeping soundly, Abby had time to think.

Riley. Emmy. Same person? Couldn't be. Maybe. Around and around, back and forth. Then it hit her.

The scar.

When they were kids, back at camp, they'd gone on a night hike. Okay, so it wasn't an official hike. They'd actually decided to go exploring on their own, up the hill to the top of Pioneer. Most of the girls who'd gone along with the harebrained scheme had gotten scared and gone back down to the cabins, but not Abby and Emmy. They planned to stay up there all night.

60

Until Pops rescued them. Pops. Abby shuddered just thinking about what a deceitful son of a bitch he actually was. And her father, to boot. God, she hoped she'd inherited nothing from his gene pool. Or passed it along to EJ.

Abby shook herself mentally, coming out of her reverie and thinking again about that scar. Emmy had been bitten by a brown recluse that night. No one even realized it until a few weeks later, but she'd been pretty sick for a couple days. Twenty years later, the scar was still there. Or had been. On her left leg, below her knee.

And really, Ab, she told herself, what are you going to do? Demand that Riley show you a scar that may or may not be there? Ask if she'd ever been bitten by a brown recluse?

Or, she supposed, she could just ask her. Huh. Simple, right? Well, she needed to make a decision, because this thinking stuff was getting old. Either Riley is Emmy or she isn't. Time for the direct approach. Probably. Maybe.

Damn.

As the sun went down, the three crawled from the rubble and approached the ruins of the Ohio Street Bridge. The moon was in and out of the clouds, making for enough light to see but perhaps not enough to be spotted if Co-OpCom was lurking about. They had to take their chances. Always keep on the move when in enemy territory.

Elizabeth wasn't improving, but she wasn't getting any worse. She seemed to constantly talk to herself, or to someone, but only her lips moved; she remained silent. The further away from the city they walked, the more stiff and awkward the girl became. Finally, after just an hour, they stopped again to allow her to rest.

Alison tried to tempt her to eat, but had no luck. She did accept water, however, and that would have to be enough for now. She hadn't seemed to recognize Alison yet, but she tolerated her.

Abby had looked her over after they first emerged from the tunnels, and could find nothing physically wrong with Elizabeth. Heaven only knows what they'd done to her mind during her captivity.

And Johnny? What had happened to him?

They finally reached Elmhurst and safety. For now.

Chapter Eight

The entire house was in an uproar when Abby and Alison arrived with Elizabeth. A quiet uproar, since one never knew who might be in the vicinity.

EJ was too well-trained to shriek when she saw her mother as she rushed outside with Storm to help the survivors. But she clung to Abby for hours afterwards. EJ was no dummy; she knew the things that grownups sometimes didn't say were as important as the things they spoke aloud.

Brad was so relieved that Alison was all right, he barely noticed that she seemed almost as excited to see the flask he'd retrieved as she was to see him. Of course, she had known all along that she was perfectly fine; he'd been the who was worried.

Riley was the only one missing from the little reunion. Tom appeared and carried Elizabeth inside where Storm could begin to assess her condition in a more thorough way than Abby had been able to in the field. Sam was already out there on guard duty, and even the restrained Lee came to greet them, Jake in tow.

But no Riley.

The entire group dispersed to do whatever it was they had to do. Abby took EJ to their quarters, and Alison and Brad followed within a few minutes, Brad hesitating as he wondered if he should say anything to Riley.

But no, Sam was heading that way now, and Riley had said she'd handle things with Abby. He only hoped that Abby wouldn't bring it up, because he wasn't completely sure that he could deceive her, if only temporarily.

He had nothing to worry about; Abby spoke very little and fell asleep soon after, EJ by her side. He really wanted to be alone with Alison for a bit, but with all this hanging over his head, he figured he was safer just not talking to anyone until it all came to light. Finally, he fell asleep too, beside Alison.

Riley was pacing again. She was well aware that those missing had returned, knew it, in fact, before the rest of the group, since Sam had seen them coming long before they reached the house and had told her first. Her mind was churning and she was all worked up, sick to her stomach and with a pending headache, which is why she'd chosen to remain in her room.

She knew she had to talk to Abby sooner rather than later. A few days was all well and good, what with everything going on, but it had been hard to remain silent during those few days, let alone to continue the charade. And Brad knew, too. That complicated things a bit. It was only a matter of time before one of them slipped up and Abby found out the wrong way.

But first, Riley had to make a decision.

Did she continue her life as Riley, rebel leader, or go back to being Emmy, the one who was concerned, always, for the welfare and comfort of others? Could she combine her two roles? Did she want to?

She knew she couldn't abandon her post here. Or her people. Never. But there was Abby . . .

Back and forth. Back and forth.

When Abby awoke, it was nearly noon. She left EJ, still sleeping soundly, and went in search of food. She grabbed a few things from the makeshift kitchen and went outside to the back porch. It was artfully sheltered from both the elements and prying eyes; not that there were any people nearby, or at least there weren't supposed to be.

She gazed out at the ruined suburbs. Nice time for her first visit to the Chicago area. Huh. She decided she didn't like it much, and it wasn't because of the bombing and the, er, hospitality down in the tunnels. It was just too crowded, much like the St. Louis 'burbs, but less familiar. Just so . . . different. Somehow.

She tensed as a board creaked behind her, and then relaxed when she realized someone had come out the back door to join her.

"Mind if I sit down?" It was Riley.

"Sure, go ahead. Your house, after all."

The silence stretched between them. Abby's tension returned a thousandfold as she tried to remain nonchalant, staring across the landscape, barely moving.

"Abby. Abby, look at me."

"No," said Abby, with a tiny smile born out of nerves. She felt like a six-year-old. But she couldn't look at Riley. She felt as though she was going to explode, as if things were changing and she wasn't going to like that change; as if she were about to get some very bad news.

Riley touched her hand, tentatively, then with a firm grip. "Abby."

Slowly, Abby turned her head and looked Riley directly in the eyes. Her mouth was dry. She studied her face, her hair. No.

She pulled her hand away and stood up to leave.

And then she looked down . . . at Emmy. No. Yes.

Her legs were shaking, and she sat down again, hard. Not possible.

"Yes, it's me, Abby. You were right all along."

She didn't believe it. Not possible. As much as she wanted to believe . . . No, Brad must have said something to this Riley, let something slip. All of it was just coincidence, and for some reason, Riley wanted her to think she was . . . No.

"I'm sorry," said Abby, her voice shaking. "You're mistaken. You must be talking about something or someone else. I can't—I can't do this. You can't be . . . she died. A long time ago."

"Abby," Emmy said gently. "It is me, I promise. I didn't die. I thought I had. I wanted to. But I wanted to come home even more . . . someday.

"Remember the first time we went to camp?"

Abby did. Of course, she did.

"Remember when we met Cal?"

Abby's hands were shaking. She couldn't speak. She dared to look at . . . Riley? Emmy? Yes. No.

"And after VADER, you came for me. When my mom died."

"No! You can't be Emmy; I don't care what you claim to remember!" Abby jumped to her feet again, ready to bolt, looking around wildly. "Emmy died. I was there. I saw it. I see it in my dreams, every single night!"

"Abby, look at this. I know you remember when it happened. Look, dammit!" Emmy was struggling to roll up the leg of her jeans. "If I'm not Emmy, how do I know about this?"

Abby looked. The scar. It was there, on Emmy's left leg.

She turned and walked away, far away, down through the yard and out to the back alley. She kept walking and didn't look back.

Robin Tidwell

Chapter Nine

BOOM!

The house shook; the windows rattled. Sam appeared on the back porch, and Riley snapped, "Get everyone downstairs now, conference room!" Sam ran back inside, and Riley scanned the horizon. She saw plumes of smoke to the north and the west. Arlington Heights. Elgin.

And she saw Abby, coming back at a run. She waited.

Abby slowly walked up the steps. She stopped in front of Emmy. No. Yes. Yes, this was Emmy. So far away and so many years later, all those years of dreaming about her death, all those nightmares. And here she was.

Abby was pissed.

Not the kind of anger when you miss your target during practice, not the kind when you know where you left a cache but can't quite remember. No, those were mere irritations. This was deep, all-encompassing anger. Why the hell didn't Emmy come back? Or send word? She obviously wasn't still a prisoner, hadn't been for years. Just up here in Chicago, carrying on, while Abby was left to mourn. Yes, she was pissed.

Emmy started to speak, but Abby held up a hand to stop her. "No. Not now. I'm furious with you. Later, we can talk.

69

You have a lot of explaining to do. A lot." She brushed past Emmy and went inside, following the others downstairs.

Emmy looked out over the horizon once more, saw the black smoke rising from the northwest, increasing in density. She turned and went inside to rally her troops.

Everyone was gathered. Abby was in the corner, talking to Storm, and refused to even glance at Emmy. Emmy sighed and got to work, struggling to hold back tears of both relief and sadness.

"All right," said Riley. "Let's get started. They're on the move again—Arlington and Elgin, and they're going south from there. If we don't hurry, we'll be caught up in the trap. Is Gene back?"

Tom shook his head. "Not yet. My lab can be ready to go in half an hour, tops."

"Good," shot back Riley, "because I'm not sure we even have that long. I'll give you fifteen minutes."

"I'm on it." Tom rushed out the door to pack his equipment.

"Sam, get on out of here and go let the folks at Joliet know we're on the way." Sam disappeared, already geared up.

"How's our patient, Storm? Can she travel?"

The older woman hesitated. "She is still not speaking, but she is eating and resting well. She appears to be quite taken with EJ, and I would be more confident if EJ could travel with us." She turned to Abby. "Would this be possible?"

"I can vouch for Storm," said Riley, "if you're worried."

"Really?" said Abby, raising a brow. "That's comforting." She looked at her daughter's eager face, and then at Storm. "Yes, she can go."

"Thanks, Mom!" EJ was clearly excited. The deciding factor, however, hadn't been Emmy's remark but Storm's peaceful countenance and the fact that Abby had every confidence in EJ's own capabilities. EJ hugged her mom and skipped off with Storm.

"All right," said Riley. "Lee, I want you to take Brad and Abby and Alison. I'll stay here and wait for Gene. Don't worry, I won't stay long, and I'll get the heck out of Dodge if they start coming closer." Lee still looked skeptical, but she motioned for the others to follow as she left the room.

Abby walked out with the rest of them, never looking back.

Emmy sat down and lowered her head onto the table. She didn't know what else she was supposed to do. She'd gotten the others out of there, she was doing her job, but Abby . . . She had to talk to her, had to make things right, to explain. But not now. They could all be blown to kingdom come at any time, and her group was the priority, not herself. Not even Abby.

Tom stuck his head in the door to check on her, and Emmy waved him off. Storm and EJ, with Elizabeth, appeared next. Sam was probably a third of the way to Joliet, and the others had left; she could hear them going out the back.

She checked the time and decided to give Gene another thirty minutes. He knew where to rendezvous. She really was just waiting here to put some distance between Abby and herself and to clean up the place. She almost laughed when she remembered the old Emmy, the one who would have pushed all the chairs back into place at the conference table and then tidied up the rest of the house.

Now, when she was cleaning up, it meant removing anything incriminating, any papers that Co-OpCom might find useful, and stray ammo or supplies. There was very little of those last two; her people had been trained to pick up and carry whatever they could use, the important things. They were almost constantly on the move in northern Illinois.

The bombs were still falling; they sounded much closer. Time to go, Gene or no Gene. Emmy hoisted her pack onto her back and went up the stairs and out the back door.

Abby was waiting.

"Tell me what happened."

Emmy looked her square in the eye. "They came for me, took me away with Pops. They kept me in a room, alive. When I was well enough to be moved, they took me to DC and operated. They made me a different person, in more ways than just my face.

"Is that enough for now? Can we go?"

Abby didn't answer for a moment. She was thinking. She reached out a hand, tentatively, and touched Emmy's cheek. Neither of them moved.

Abby cried.

They went south on York Street out of Elmhurst. The noise from the choppers and their falling payloads made conversation difficult, but that was probably best. Each was lost in thought and maneuvered through the rubble-filled streets almost automatically. Abby was concerned for EJ, even though she'd put on a brave face earlier, but she realized that any place to get bombed to smithereens was the same as the next: the safe house, here, somewhere between. At least it would be quick.

Joliet was thirty miles away; the others should arrive before Abby and Emmy. In the meantime, staying alive was becoming a higher priority. Co-OpCom had started in the north and the west, but was rapidly raining down destruction in a southern sweep.

They stopped to take a break after two hours, crouching in the shadows of a building that had been lost long before today's attack.

"They're coming out of O'Hare," Emmy told her.

"What difference does that make?" asked Abby.

"It's a big deal. They kept Midway open as it was smaller and easier to patrol, and O'Hare was pretty much left alone. We've done some reconnaissance up there. Had some good plans, too, but I guess those are off the table now. Damn."

"You've been busy," remarked Abby. She looked at her old friend curiously. The old Emmy, completely capable in all manner of self-defense methods, a good shot, and able to live in the outdoors for long periods of time, nevertheless was a much gentler person than Abby. More willing to give others the benefit of the doubt. More hesitant before shooting someone. And much, much less likely to plan or carry out the destruction of a corrupt government.

By nine o'clock they'd reached Bolingbrook. Emmy led Abby near the house where she'd initially directed them several days ago, but they stopped half a block down the street. The bombs hadn't yet reached this far and, in truth, had stopped several hours ago. Co-opCom pilots always had been wusses when it came to nighttime operations.

"Just had a thought," whispered Emmy. "Follow me."

This was a twist on their old relationship, Abby thought wryly. But she complied, of course. This was a new Emmy, in charge and well-respected, and Abby decided she could get used to this.

There were lights on in the safe house. And no guards posted. They waited, listening to the voices to determine how many were inside. Abby held up three fingers. Emmy nodded. She recognized those voices. That traitor, Brenda, and two men from her cell up north. She wanted answers, and she was going to get them.

She motioned for Abby to go around back as she crept towards the front door. Sig in her left hand, AR-15 in her right, both weapons ready to fire. No point in being subtle. She kicked in the door and came through in almost the same motion.

Voices were stilled, and everyone froze. After that, it got complicated.

Abby came in through the back, silently and with deadly purpose. Co-opCom or someone else, Emmy had indicated they were dangerous and most likely the enemy. That was good enough for Abby.

Sadly, she was a bit late to the game. As she heard the door break down, she knew all bets were off and silence was no longer an issue. She came into the front room as Emmy had pinned the three miscreants in the corner and was steadily aiming her assault rifle. Used to being the one in charge, Abby quite enjoyed seeing Emmy handle the situation.

"All right, Brenda, what the hell? You managed to get a number of good men killed in the last couple days, yet here you are, safe and sound. I ought to shoot you just for target practice."

"Riley, I swear, it's not like that! We, uh, heard about movement from Co-OpCom and just got out of our house right before they struck."

"Oh, yeah? And how'd you hear they were coming?" Emmy tapped her foot impatiently, waiting for the answer, which Brenda appeared unwilling to provide. Her loss.

Emmy fired. Brenda slumped against the wall and slid to the floor, her body jerking spasmodically for a few short seconds. "Next?" said Emmy.

One of the men was staring at Brenda's remains, clearly in shock; his mouth moved, but no words came out. The other, shorter and heavier, stared at the floor and shifted nervously.

"Well?" demanded Emmy. "I don't have all night. Spill it, Freddie."

Freddie spilled it. Emmy shot him, too.

"Nate? Any last words?"

He had none. He joined Brenda on the floor, full of holes.

"Let's go," said Emmy, turning and walking out the door.

Robin Tidwell

Chapter Ten

Jules and Mario strolled hand in hand down Cherokee Street. Jules briefly wondered what it had been like back in the old days, with all the shops and the people just living normal, everyday lives. Then again, walking around somewhat leisurely in broad daylight was a novelty in itself. The north-side gangs had been quiet for several days, and while Mario was alert, there was no real danger. Today.

She'd spent last night in the women's quarters. Not as archaic as it sounded, it was a dormitory-style room for any unattached women in the family. Jules only remembered one of them, Dacia, who'd been a part of their last assault against Co-OpCom.

Mario had come for her early this morning, and they were on their way to see Father Timothy. Since there was no license, no registry, Jules wasn't quite sure of the point to this exercise, but she loved Mario, and if this is what he wanted, it was okay with her. Not a deal-breaker. She thought just being with him was fine, too, like her mom and Brad. Not much difference.

Father Timothy lived in the shell of St. Matthews on Jefferson Street. Technically, it was outside of the area of Mario's protection, but no one bothered him. And it bothered

Father Timothy not in the least that he made his home in the basement of a Protestant denomination's building.

Mario knocked on the door. Father Timothy appeared, disheveled as usual, reeling slightly from a late night spent wrestling with his demons.

"Mario, my son! What brings you to my humble abode so early on such a beautiful morning?"

"I want you to meet Jules," said Mario. "We'd like to be married."

"Married? Married?" cried the priest. "In this day and age? Of course, I'd be delighted to perform the nuptials!" Father Timothy had rarely officiated at weddings since Co-OpCom had taken over. It was more common for couples to simply live together until one or the other became bored and moved on.

He dragged the young couple inside and moved some stacks of papers off two chairs so they could sit down. He looked at them and smiled happily, like a child, as he clapped his hands together in joy.

"Now, tell me, in detail, why the two of you wish to be married."

Mario and Jules looked at each other for a moment, surprised at the question. It seemed obvious to them.

"Because we love each other!" declared Mario.

Father Timothy looked at Jules. "And you, young lady? Do you love him as well?"

Jules nodded.

"Wonderful," said Father Timothy. "Now, let us determine if you are compatible in other ways."

"Father," said Mario, "no offense, but is all this really necessary?"

"Of course, my boy! I haven't officiated at a wedding in a very long time, but in the old days you would have to attend counseling for many weeks before being allowed to be married. I'm merely giving you the abbreviated version, on account of our changed circumstances.

"Jules, my dear, are you a Catholic?"

"Um, no, Father."

"Hmmm," the priest said. "That is a problem." He pondered for a moment. "And one which we can solve! I take it you've never been baptized?"

"No," said Jules, looking a bit uncomfortable.

"Well, then," Father Timothy told her, "we'll have to take care of that before the ceremony. So, assuming you both are, or will be, Catholic, let's start with the things you have in common. Mario?"

Mario looked at Jules. Then he looked at the priest.

Father Timothy sighed. "Mario, I know exactly what you have done over the years and what you continue to do. Tell me, Jules, are you involved in this as well?"

"Yes, Father, I am," she said, rather defiantly.

"Very well. So you have guns and bombs and anti-government sentiment in common." He winked. "I've had more couples come to me with much less compatibility, so we move on. What about children?"

"Children?" said Jules, aghast. "Children?"

"Well, yes," answered Father Timothy. "They are often a consequence of marriage, after all."

Jules tightened her grip on Mario's hand. This wasn't something she'd considered. She was beginning to realize that maybe she hadn't quite thought this through.

Mario spoke up. "Yes, Father, I suppose someday we will have children. And I will raise them in the faith, just as I was taught." He squeezed Jules' hand.

Father Timothy looked at Jules. "And you, my dear? Would you agree to raise the children as good Catholics?"

Jules had no idea what this entailed, but Mario smiled reassuringly at her, and she nodded.

"Excellent!" said the priest. "Mario, will you step outside, please? I wish to speak with Jules regarding her baptism."

"Yes, Father." Mario whispered to Jules and squeezed her hand once more before walking outside.

"Jules, my dear, do you know anything at all about our religion? About the Holy Father or His Son?"

"No, Father."

"So, we start at the beginning . . ."

An hour later, Father Timothy brought Mario back inside and seated him next to Jules. "Your fiancée has learned much today, Mario. Now, my boy, we can proceed with the ceremony."

Jules wiped a stray drop of water off her forehead and smiled at Mario. She was relieved that the priest's homily on the Church hadn't been as horrific as she'd imagined, and the baptism wasn't as bad either. She hadn't been sure quite what to expect, but she'd learned more than she realized over years of studying, even if she hadn't been to school—or church, for that matter.

"Mario, Jules, have you come here freely and without reservation to give yourselves to each other in marriage? Will you love and honor each other as man and wife for the rest of your lives? Will you accept children lovingly from God and bring them up according to the law of Christ and His Church?"

And so they were married.

They walked happily back to the old brewery, hand in hand, with Father Timothy trailing behind them. The women of Mario's family had prepared a wedding lunch, and all but those on guard duty were present. Jules didn't at all miss the frilly accoutrements of a traditional wedding, since she'd never seen one or even actually thought about it all. She did, however, think of her mother and wondered how things were going in Chicago.

***

Alison and Brad, led by Lee, reached the safe house in Joliet. The bombing had all but ceased, although they could still see black plumes of smoke rising to the north. Lee introduced them to Dave, the cell leader in that area, and he turned them over to Bart, who showed them to their quarters.

The house was set up much like Stefanie and Carmine's had been in St. Louis. It was actually four houses, connected via tunnels, which appeared abandoned on the surface but were quite large and well-appointed. This was the base of the entire operation, with Riley at its head, in the Chicago area.

Tom had already arrived and was setting up his equipment and research materials; Brad went to see if he could help. Alison went into the war room with Lee, who was plotting the next phase of the multi-pronged attack on Co-OpCom.

Lee went to the map wall and showed Alison their current location, along with those of the cells spread across the area: Munster, Roseland, Orland Park, and Warrenville.

"What's the plan?" asked Alison.

"Riley will go over it in more detail when she arrives, but in general we've been trying to cut off supplies and transport to Co-opCom. Mostly we're just harassing them, since we don't have the numbers or the firepower to do much else.

"Specifically, we plan to get inside the city, infiltrate key positions, and assassinate the president."

Alison thought for a moment. "What about his VP? If the president is gone, that dumbass will take over. I mean, he's pretty old, but still—he could cause even worse problems that we have now."

Lee gave her a hard look. "That was phase one. He's been dead for six months."

Storm and EJ arrived safely, with Elizabeth in tow. She hadn't caused any problems whatsoever, and she seemed to be gaining strength as well as becoming more alert. She'd stopped muttering to herself, but still wouldn't speak directly to anyone.

Gene was the next to reach the safe house. He'd stopped in Elmhurst on his way, just before the bombs came raining down on the house there, but hadn't seen anyone else. He'd hightailed on down to Joliet.

Sam came in from guard duty and went to catch some sleep. She'd been up for 24 hours by now and was about to crash. They promised to wake her as soon as Riley and Abby arrived. Dave gathered everyone in the main room to discuss the next move, pending Riley's arrival.

***

Emmy and Abby were slowly working their way south from Bolingbrook. After the incident with Brenda and her cohorts, Abby was even more astounded at the changes in Emmy. When they stopped for a break, just inside a wooded area, Abby was ready to hear more of her friend's story.

"So what happened after your surgery?"

Emmy looked away from Abby, gazing up into the sky as she stretched her muscles.

"First," she said, "you should know that Pops told me you were dead. He came to visit me just before they took me away from St. Louis."

"Bastard," said Abby, with venom.

Emmy looked at her, wondering if there was more to that expletive, but didn't pursue it. "I found out later that it wasn't true, that you were alive and they were trying to find you. They used certain . . . methods on me to get the answers they wanted.

"I never told them a thing."

Abby scooted over next to Emmy and took her hand. "I never would have thought that."

"After Washington, they brought me here, to Chicago. They set me up in a penthouse over on Michigan Avenue. I was supposed to make nice with all the big shots. Even the president himself." Here she stopped. She hoped Abby knew what she meant; she prayed she wouldn't have to talk about it in any detail. Just saying this much had about done her in. All traces of Riley had disappeared in the telling, and she was finished.

Abby put her arms around Emmy and held her tightly for a long time.

At last, they helped each other to their feet and began the last leg of the trip to Joliet.

Robin Tidwell

Chapter Eleven

Abby and Riley finally arrived, and Alison came to greet them. She appeared to be puzzled as she looked from Riley to Abby and back again, but she made no comment. Riley told her they'd meet her in the conference room in just a few minutes.

As Abby began to follow Alison, Emmy stopped her. "No one here knows about my past. Not all of it. Leave it to me. There might be questions, and there might be some things you don't want to hear, but trust me, Abby. I have to do this, and it has to be now, and it has to be done my way.

"I've been with these people for five years, and they don't know all of it either. They know me as Riley, the woman who was once on the side of the government and defected. Today, right now, they're going to learn the whole story. I can't say what will happen after that." She smiled crookedly. "They may ask me to leave."

Abby nodded. She was ready for anything, but mostly she was ready to be done with the mystery and to be able to reclaim her friendship with Emmy. Ten long years.

They were all waiting when Riley walked to the head of the conference table. "I have something to tell you all," she began.

"Something you may not like, something that may change the way you see things. And me."

She looked around the table at each of them before speaking again, with no trace of emotion. Cold and hard.

"Before I came here from DC, I lived in Missouri. With Abby. And Brad. We hid from Co-opCom for years, since VADER, and we lost many good people along the way. Oh, yes, we fought them. We went into St. Louis; we infiltrated their offices; we blew up their buildings.

"Then they made their final push to flush us out, to kill us. That day, they bombed our sanctuary, our refuge. I was trying to get one of our men out, along with our friend Ted, and the building took a direct hit. The next thing I knew, I was being airlifted out. My name was . . . Emmy."

She paused and took a drink of water. Her audience was still and silent, taking in every word.

"They took me to St. Louis and to DC. They kept me alive, and then they changed me. I know you've seen the scars. They didn't waste any top surgeons on me; I was just someone they could use until they were tired of me. I had to be at least presentable, you see, because . . . because of the work they assigned me."

Abby didn't want to hear any more. It was bad enough, reliving this, seeing the looks on everyone's faces. Alison's jaw had dropped; Brad was looking at the floor. She was thankful that EJ wasn't in the room. The rest of the group, those who had worked with Riley for several years, appeared to be dumbfounded. No one looked angry; no one challenged her. Abby was grateful for that, too.

"They told me that Abby was dead. Later, they altered their stories and questioned me over and over, trying to get me to tell them her location. I refused, in spite of . . ." Her voice broke for just a moment; then she continued. "In spite of the torture. This is why they had to - to change me.

"This is why Abby didn't know who I was, not really." She tried to smile. "And this is why we've paid close attention to St. Louis, and to any rebels still there. Because of Abby, and Brad, although I didn't know they were still alive, after all these years. Not until George came to us. He told me about them."

Tom nodded. He remembered when George first found them, about six months ago. He'd almost gotten himself shot. He'd been on his way to the city, scouting out the suburbs and preparing to bring a group up here to investigate Co-opCom. That's when they'd learned of the rebels in St. Louis, and he'd mentioned Abby specifically. Tom remembered, too, that Riley had questioned the man in depth and had had several long conversations with him.

"There's more," said Emmy. "I had to . . . entertain a lot. Even the president, once or twice. And then . . ." Her voice broke for a moment. "And then, I decided that I was either going to die or escape.

"The vice president visited me often. He was just as clueless as we'd always suspected, even before VADER, and he loved to talk, especially about things that he shouldn't be repeating. But, you see, he didn't view me as a person, let alone anyone who could do anything.

"So I smiled and nodded a lot. And paid attention.

"And then, I escaped."

Lee was staring at the floor, lost in thought. Sure, this was all plausible, but really—why did Riley, or Emmy, or whoever she was, stay in Chicago with Co-opCom so long? It had been what, two years? Three?

Alison was still sitting there with her mouth hanging open, taking in every word. Abby had tears in her eyes, and even

Brad looked a little weepy. Sam was openly crying. The others, Dave and Bart and the rest of them, looked anywhere but directly at Emmy.

Gene was the first to react.

He went to Emmy and put his arm around her. He stared at each of them for a moment before speaking.

"This lady saved my hide on more than one occasion. She's got my complete trust, and whatever she did in the past has no bearing on today. I'm betting that some of you have stories too, ones you haven't told us for whatever reason, and that doesn't mean we trust you less." He turned to Emmy.

"Riley, Emmy, whatever you want to be called, I'm proud to be on your side, and I'm staying right here with you."

There was a brief, almost imperceptible moment of silence, and then, one by one, each person in the room pledged to remain under Emmy's command.

Emmy herself was struggling to maintain her composure, but quickly got a grip on her emotions. They had to work to do, and it was still up to her. Later, she could relax, but for now, the situation demanded her full attention.

"Thank you," said Emmy, with feeling. "I appreciate each and every one of you, and I promise to uphold the vow I made when I first came here: to stop Co-OpCom.

"Now, let's begin. As necessary as my story was for you to hear, we've taken up too much valuable time. Gene, what's the situation?"

"I went up to Norwood Park, where we'd heard Brenda had moved. She wasn't there, and two of her men were missing as well. The others were dead."

They digested this in silence.

"You know what that means as well I do," Gene went on, "but since I had no clue as to which direction they went, I did some more reconnaissance. Went over to O'Hare for a bit. Co-OpCom has a whole big operation set up there. I didn't go in too close, or stay very long, but I know that much. It's huge.

"Came on back down here and saw the bombing off to the west. Looks like they're finishing what they started a few years ago. They quit when it got dark, as usual. Candy-asses." He rolled his eyes in disgust.

"No worries about Brenda, Gene. Abby and I came across her and her men in Bolingbrook."

"What did she say?" asked Lee. "Did she tell you what happened?"

"No time to talk," Emmy said. "And she won't be answering anyone now. Neither will the other two." She shrugged. "So, the question is where do we go from here?" She took two long strides to the map wall.

"The north side is gone. The Loop is where everything is congregated, a pretty small area. They haven't yet gotten to the south side, but that could be tomorrow, or the next day. We need to move fast.

"Our original plan still stands, except we have extra bodies now." She glanced at Abby. "Unless there are any objections?" No one spoke.

"All right, then, let's get some sleep, and we'll all report back here at 0600."

Robin Tidwell

Chapter Twelve

As they left the room, each stopped to speak briefly with Emmy. Abby, Brad, and Alison remained behind.

"Mind clueing us in on this 'plan' of yours?" asked Brad. He was a little overwhelmed with Emmy's story, but not skeptical. He knew what Co-opCom was capable of doing. He was, however, concerned about a plan of which he knew nothing at all. While he was willing to die, he was unwilling to take unnecessary risks based on a foolhardy decision.

"Not at all," Emmy replied. "Let me show you." She pointed to the map. "We're about 30 miles from Midway. That's where the government bigwigs fly in and out and where most of their military is based. But we're not quite 50 miles from O'Hare, and that's our target.

"Co-opCom never used it until now because Midway was closer and much smaller—easier to patrol and defend, if necessary. Fortunately for us, O'Hare was once a manufacturing plant for C-54s and was also, for a few decades, an Air Reserve Station. We've found lots of goodies up there that we've been storing and cataloging."

"Well, damn," said Brad. "Guess that's lost to us now."

"Not necessarily," said Emmy, with a twinkle in her eye. "We have plans for that too! But back to what we're discussing: Chicago itself. We have it on good authority that the president's top aide is coming to town in two days. We plan to give General Scott a warm welcome. A very warm welcome."

"What? Who?" Alison jumped to her feet. "That bitch!"

"I take it you know her?" asked Emmy.

Alison was so mad she was sputtering and was practically incoherent. Brad jumped in to translate. "Yeah, back when Alison was working for the government, she had a few run-ins with Kat, and then again in St. Louis, before we came up here."

Emmy looked worried. "You were working for Co-OpCom?"

"Well, yes. But only because the pay was good and I was an idiot. Brad here straightened me out, in a roundabout way, which is how we met." Alison waved her hands in excitement. "But you have got to let me get first crack at Kat!"

"Well . . ." Emmy looked doubtful. "Since Brad and Abby can vouch for you . . . But some of the others? After my little announcement earlier, they might be uncomfortable. To say the least."

"Em," Abby interjected, "Alison is Juliet's mother."

Emmy was speechless for a moment.

"But . . . what? How?"

Alison sighed, exasperated. "The usual way. Sex. With her father, may his soul rot in hell. Now, can we get back to Chicago and Kat?"

"Fine," said Emmy. She wasn't entirely enthralled with this Alison person. But she had a job to do. She pointed back to the map.

"The first team will go in here, at Midway. Their job is to observe and track. The second team will be a welcoming committee of sorts for General Scott, downtown at the Daley Center. I'm assuming, Alison, that you want to be part of the second team?"

"Yes!" Alison nearly shouted.

"Okay, then. The three of you will go with me. Gene is commanding the first team, and I'll be in radio contact with him. We'll leave tomorrow at noon, and I'll cover everything in detail when we all meet in the morning."

Alison and Brad left the room, Alison practically dancing down the corridor. She patted her pocket and found her flask. Definitely time for a celebratory shot of tequila!

Abby went to Emmy, who had sat down quite suddenly and looked rather pale. "Em?"

Emmy smiled faintly. "I'm fine, just worn out. After all the excitement lately, and reliving my little tale . . . and you're here now . . . I'm just tired."

"Come on," said Abby, hauling Emmy to her feet. "I'll tuck you in before I go see EJ. Just like old times."

She made sure Emmy was nearly sleeping before she went in search of her daughter, who was, as she suspected, bunking with Storm. And Elizabeth.

She sat next to EJ and stroked her hair, only half-listening to EJ's chatter. This precious daughter of hers - so young, so strong, but always in the line of danger. Abby sighed. Maybe someday it would be different. Maybe.

"And Mom, guess what? We get to go stay in the old prison! Sam's going to take us there tomorrow, and we'll be safe, so you won't have to worry so much."

"Prison?" asked Abby, with a smile at EJ's imagination.

"No, really! Mom, it's way cool. They say it's even haunted!"

"EJ, my love, I think you exaggerate a bit."

Storm smiled as she listened to their conversation, while busily tending to Elizabeth. The poor girl still needed to be spoon-fed, and Storm was beginning to think she might never recover.

"That one," she indicated EJ, "surely has an active imagination. But in this case, she is correct. The old Joliet prison is just two streets over, and Sam has prepared a place for us to stay until this is all finished."

Abby was startled, but upon quick reflection thought that it was probably an excellent place to hole up - provided, of course, that one could escape more easily than the former prisoners. She kissed her daughter goodnight and went back to Emmy's room.

Her old friend was awake, waiting for her.

"You're supposed to be sleeping," Abby told her.

"I'm not tired," said Emmy, rather like a child.

"Yes, you are," Abby scolded. It was, indeed, like old times.

"I want to talk."

"About? Busy day tomorrow, Em, and while I'm getting used to your new role here, and think you're doing a fabulous job, now is not the time to lose it—or lose sleep."

"Tell me what happened after they took me away."

"Hell of a bedtime story you picked," said Abby crossly.

"Fine," said Emmy as she rolled over, facing the wall.

Abby sighed. She knew Emmy wouldn't let it go; she'd speak up again as soon as Abby was dozing off. Old habits die hard.

"I took Juliet and ran, just as you said to do. We went up the hill and circled back to the cave. We lived there for six months, just the two of us. And then Noah showed up."

Emmy raised up on one arm. "Noah? He's alive?"

Abby's gut tightened as she remembered how sick Juliet had been, how Noah had used up the last of his medicine and, when the illness came upon him, had been too weak to fight it.

"No," she said shortly.

Emmy laid back down. "And he's EJ's father, yes?"

"Yes."

"Go on."

"We stayed there for ten years. And then Co-OpCom started sniffing around. More precisely, Brad. He knew we'd been there, and with the brainwashing by dear old Pops, he was coming after us. Alison had just transferred from Chicago. She was in his squad.

"She was about fed up with government tactics, and she was really annoyed with Brad. What did she call him? Oh, yeah—Major Creepy. Her vocabulary has, er, expanded since then. Anyway, Brad had a breakdown, breakthrough, whatever you want to call it, almost as soon as he got to the camp gates. Then they came looking for me, but I'd taken the girls and left camp right before they arrived. Had a feeling, and I'd seen some activity . . . and I didn't know it was Brad at the time."

"Long story short, I was up in Franklin County. Brad remembered the place, and once he convinced Alison that he wasn't the bogeyman, they came up there. I damn near shot them both before I recognized him."

"And Juliet?" asked Emmy. "She must be 18 now, or close to it. The last time I saw her, she was the same age as EJ."

"Yes. As you know, she's in St. Louis. Fancies herself in love with this Mario guy. Alison and I aren't thrilled about it, but you know kids." Abby shrugged.

Emmy tried not to laugh. She really did. Back in the old days, even though Abby worked with teenagers, it was hysterically funny to her to hear all this motherly concern.

"I just hope," Abby added, tossing a pillow at Emmy, who was giggling, "that she doesn't do anything stupid."

***

Stupid, thought Jules. I was really dumb. Oh, stop talking to yourself, she almost said aloud. She looked around to see if anyone was nearby. She tried again to get the paper on the cloth in the correct position and keep it there while she pinned it. A study in concentration, she didn't realize Mario had walked up behind her until he touched her shoulder.

Yelping, Jules jumped and turned in one smooth motion and reached for her knife - which was lying across the room on an old dresser.

Mario swept her into his arms and tossed her on the bed, tickling her until she begged for mercy.

"So how are the sewing lessons coming?" he asked, as they lay together companionably.

"Huh," said Jules. "I can't believe I lost that bet with you and now I'm stuck here doing this stuff! I hate this, I can't do it, and I'd much rather be with you."

"Soon, Jules. Just be patient."

"Ha! Patient? Nope, not me, not at all. Besides, why do I need to learn this? I can mend, I can sew on buttons—and they usually stay on, at least for a few days. This is . . . this is stupid!"

Mario smiled. His new wife was not very domestic, but he'd known that as soon as they met. And, while he was just a few years older than she, he sometimes felt like her father. In the week since their wedding, they'd clashed more than a few times, hence Jules' current predicament.

But he wasn't angry, and he cleared his throat, about to speak, when Jules stopped him.

"Oh, no, you don't! You are not going to let me out of this. When I lose, I lose, and I take the consequences. I'm going to finish this dress if it kills me!" And, she thought to herself, if I actually have to wear it, it might well kill me! Ugh.

"Very well," said Mario. "But I'm going to be gone for several days, scouting upriver. I thought you might want to come along, but, well . . ."

Jules tossed a pillow at him, and soon they were involved in quite the wrestling match. It was a draw until they fell off the bed and landed hard on the floor, but at that point, neither of them noticed.

Mario went upriver with his men later that evening. Jules stayed behind. It was the best decision she ever made, and the worst.

Robin Tidwell

Chapter Thirteen

Abby went with Sam the next morning to take EJ, Storm, and Elizabeth over to the old Joliet prison. Not a bad hideout, she admitted to herself, and congratulated Sam on the setup. She kissed EJ and spoke gently to Elizabeth before going outside with Storm for a few minutes before she had to leave them.

"What's wrong with Elizabeth?" she asked.

Storm hesitated, gathering her thoughts. "I believe it's a self-induced catatonia, based on guilt over her own actions and perhaps her failure to help her brother. I don't know the story, as she has not yet spoken of it, but based on what we know of Co-OpCom, I'm quite sure it was very traumatic."

"Will she recover?" asked Abby bluntly. Her heart bled for the young girl, not quite fifteen years old, so scared and damaged.

"I don't know. I've seen a number of cases such as this. Some fully recover; others do not."

Abby went back to the safe house, where everyone was busy loading up gear and checking weapons. She took care of her own, as always, making sure her knife was sharp and she had plenty of extra ammo. Sam had provided her with a package of C4 as well.

She tried to put Elizabeth out of her mind, but she was very concerned about traveling with the girl in her present condition. She seemed compliant, at least, but Abby wondered what was going to become of her. First, however, they had a mission to carry out. And, too, there was always a possibility that she herself wouldn't make it back. Then she'd have nothing to worry about regarding Elizabeth.

So. Back to the task at hand. Never in a million years would she have thought she'd be a rebel against the government. Sure, things had been going downhill since before VADER was unleashed, but they were always small things, things that gave one pause but caused no real hardship.

Food prices soared; salaries decreased; health care was all but nonexistent and, when it could be obtained, prohibitively expensive. The only ones making money were politicians and lobbyists. And the president. Especially after the laws were amended to grant him not only a third term, but a lifetime appointment.

Abby wasn't particularly affected, as a single woman with no children and a stable job, but after she met with Cal in the park one day, she began to see the writing on the wall. As a group, she and Cal and the others purchased quantities of supplies, including weapons and ammo, and commissioned some rather unique features on a fleet of black trucks. They arranged to meet, when it became necessary, at the old camp where they'd first become friends.

And then, things got much worse.

Ultratron and Co-OpCom partnered to create a devastating virus, known as VADER, named after its creator. The goal was to eliminate certain groups of people, groups whose thinking was diametrically opposed to that of the government. VADER was a success in that it did indeed reduce the population— nearly all of it, in fact—but it also affected those who were aligned with Co-OpCom. Mercenaries were called in to help keep the peace, but mostly were used for crowd control.

The ultimate crowd control: death.

For those who survived VADER, there was a choice to be made: loss of freedom, but a nominally safe life, or go on the run, hiding out, avoiding the patrols that were sent out regularly to round up the insurgents. For Abby and the others, there was no choice.

Those who remained in the cities for safety's sake were certain they'd made the best choice. There was work for everyone, even if it was personally unsatisfying, and free food, free medical care, no guns except for those of the pseudo-military, and in general about as close to utopia as one could get, if one was able to function as a robot and barely entertain an original thought.

Of course, there was a price to pay. Food shortages were rampant; genetically modified products took the place of healthier alternatives. Sickness and death arrived frequently. Older people suffered less, in many ways, as they were lined up for euthanasia. Fewer babies were born, as Co-OpCom considered them a drain on the economy, and after all, this new country was all about choice. Government-mandated choice, of course.

And so during the years when Abby and Juliet lived in the cave down at the camp, the population began to succumb to disease and illness. Few children survived and grew up to take the place of workers who began to age out of the system and were exterminated. Control of the nation's cities shifted to DC and Chicago, with much smaller areas in Miami and LA still nominally functioning. The rest of the country was a wasteland.

Those who fled, however, either to hide or to fight another day, were growing stronger and more numerous. Some had moved into the abandoned cities and were attempting to rebuild. Others had set up their own communities in the mountains or along the southern part of the East Coast and other places where they'd never be found.

Abby knew things could never return to normal, but she was trying her best to stop the madness and to ensure that things couldn't get any worse.

And so they left Joliet, heading into Chicago.

The radio crackled to life. "Emmy? Gene. They've landed, and just as we suspected, the security is much too tight here. She's coming your way."

Emmy turned to the others as she clicked off the radio. "Okay, let's go over this one more time. The chopper from Midway is scheduled to land here, on the Great Lawn." She sketched a rough map in the thick dust on the floor of the Chicago Public Library where they were waiting. "The Daley Center is here, just five blocks west.

"General Scott will be taken there by motorcade, so we have to move fast." Emmy checked her watch. "The chopper should set down in three minutes, and then we have probably five minutes for her to do a meet and greet and get in the limo; another five to go down Washington.

"Everyone ready? All right, let's move!"

Slipping out a side door, Alison and Brad blended into the crowd and went east on Washington. Abby and Emmy walked north, then turned west onto Randolph, circling behind the old Macy's store. They stopped in the shadow of an old, falling-down theater.

Emmy pointed up. Abby could see the sharpshooters stationed across rooftops. Dearborn was blocked off by soldiers, so they backtracked to State Street. Abby was surprised by the crowds, but Emmy could have told her that this was likely a command performance. No one took holidays off anymore, but workers would be released to attend the arrival of a top government officer; of course, they would be ordered to return to their jobs immediately after.

They settled into position at the corner of Washington, under the broken clock on the corner of the Macy's building.

Alison and Brad had reached Washington as well, and moved along with the crowd near the edge of the street. They split up, Brad crossing the street, and moved on toward the former CBS building. Within minutes, the motorcade was in sight.

Since they had no way of toting around assault weapons or even .22s, here in the heart of Co-OpCom, Alison had to rely on her position; as promised, she was getting first crack at the general. Whether the shot hit or missed, Alison knew the risks: immediate takedown by the dozens of bodyguards or hundreds of mercenaries lining the rooftops. Or all of them.

And this was certainly a risk she was willing to take. She put all other thoughts out of her head as she focused on the car in which Kat most likely was riding. No clear shot there, but she'd be ready when that bitch stepped outside.

Alison and Kat had once been coworkers, both near the top of the Chicago command. Kat, however, was a true believer, and ruthless. After being accepted as a marginal member of Alison's group of friends and acquaintances, she betrayed Alison's closest friends, Eric and Marta, who were subsequently tortured and murdered. Shortly after that incident, Kat was promoted and Alison was transferred to St. Louis, presumably as punishment for her association with enemies of the state.

After Kat attained her present rank, she was sent to St. Louis to replace Colonel Hoefer. Sadly for Alison, she never got the chance to confront her former colleague before Abby and Stefanie watched Kat die—a suicide, or so they thought. But Kat left a note for Alison, a week later:

"Dear Alison, I see you made it this far. Too bad it was for nothing. I win!"

Dear Kat, thought Alison, you were wrong—this time, I win! And she watched the limo as it came to a stop in front of the Daley Center.

Alison moved closer to the curb. She could see, out of the corner of her eye, Brad watching from across the street, but her attention was focused on the woman exiting the vehicle. Suddenly, there was a loud pop, and people began screaming. Alison could see Kat stagger before the bodyguards surrounded her, and she looked down at her hand.

The Ruger was gone.

Seconds later, she was knocked to the ground as burly men dressed all in black tackled the older gentleman standing next to her. Her Ruger fell out of his hand, dropping to the pavement, and she heard the rattle of his death throes. She lifted her head and saw no fewer than a dozen bullet holes riddling his body, but she had heard nothing - nothing but the screams of the crowd as hundreds of people stampeded over and around her.

Alison struggled to her feet, knowing that if she remained on the ground, she'd be trampled to death. She scanned the crowd for Brad, in vain. Trying to get her bearings, she was shoved along with the sea of people, all trying to escape.

She had to get back to the library, just a few blocks away, but she was all turned around and no idea which way the crowd was moving. Finally, she saw an opening and pushed her way through. As she reached the old clock outside of the Macy's building, she began to run.

When she arrived at the side door of the library, the others were waiting. Brad swept her into his arms and held her tight for a moment before demanding, "Well? What happened?"

"I don't know!" Alison frowned. "I was in position, I had the gun in my hand, and then it was gone and the man next to me was on the ground and Kat was covered by her guards. Dammit."

Brad looked at Emmy. "It's safe to say that we aren't the only ones operating around here."

Emmy shrugged. "Not much we can do about it, although I wish they'd leave it to us. Or join us. Unless, of course, they can succeed. Doesn't matter who brings down Co-OpCom, but we could do without the interference."

"It's clear," said Abby, watching the alley. "Let's move out now, while we can. We can debrief later, kids. Come on!"

They planned to go north on Garland, slip around past Millennium Park, and go south to Roseland, to meet up with Gene and his squad. The street was blocked at the next corner by an ever-growing contingent of well-armed soldiers. They ducked into the entrance of an old department store to reassess.

"Can't go north, so we'll go south," said Alison. "If we can make it to Madison, there's an old subway station there. We can follow it all the way to Chinatown, out of sight. Well, if it hasn't collapsed."

Brad looked a little green around the gills. He was no fan of being below the earth.

"All right," Emmy said decisively.

They went south.

Robin Tidwell

Chapter Fourteen

Jules stretched and yawned, rolling over in bed. She opened her eyes and wondered if Mario would be back today. He'd been gone three days.

She sat up and looked across the room at her finished project. That damned dress. She'd worked hard on it, but had decided definitively that sewing was not her thing. At all. And she intended to let Mario know that, too!

She heard a commotion down in the street below and went to the window to look out. A dozen of the men were milling around, some of the women were coming outside as well, and the noise was growing louder. She threw on some clothes and ran downstairs and onto the front porch.

Bruno saw her and strode quickly to her side, taking her arm and pulling her back indoors. "It's bad," he told her. "Wait here." He left her then, alone for but a moment before two of the women came inside to sit with her. Their silence frightened her, but not as much as their sympathetic faces.

"What is it?" demanded Jules. "What's happened? Where's Mario?"

"Hush," said Rosa, taking her hand. "Everything will be okay."

Adrienne let the curtain fall and came to sit next to Jules. "Bruno is coming back. With Father Timothy."

"Someone tell me what's going on!" Jules was shaking and her palms were wet. When the priest entered the room and she saw the look on his face, she knew.

They buried Mario the next day, in the old military cemetery at Jefferson Barracks. A soldier to the end, he'd defended his squad until a bullet took him in the head. He was the last to fall, except for the one man who'd brought back the news. He had been questioned by Bruno.

Jules appeared to be calm and controlled and somewhat in a state of shock. On the inside, she was seething. Her Mario, her love, lay dead in the ground. They'd had such a short time together, barely a week. And now he was gone. She hoped that Bruno had gotten some answers.

If not, she intended to find out herself.

As soon as the service was over, she insisted that Rosa and Adrienne take her to the brewery, to Mario's office. Bruno was waiting.

"Well? What did you find out?" demanded Jules.

Bruno looked uncomfortable and he hesitated to reply, knowing that an outburst from Jules would be forthcoming. But he followed orders well. "Josiah knew about the attack. His cousin was part of it."

"I want to see him, to talk to him . . . to ask him . . ." Always strong, Jules' voice trailed off. What did it matter? Mario was dead.

"*E stato curato*," Bruno told her gently. "I have already taken care of him."

That helped a little, yes, it did, but Jules was ready for vengeance. "And now, we'll go after the rest of them."

"Mario would not have wanted you to do this, Jules. You leave them to the rest of us. I have men ready to go at a moment's notice." Bruno's job had been to protect Mario and, since the wedding, his wife as well. This is why he hadn't been on the trip upriver; he had been ordered to remain with Jules. He had no ill will toward her, but now he had a chance to avenge his boss's death, and Jules would have to remain behind. He couldn't protect her adequately while trying to kill as many of the enemy as possible. And he intended to do just that.

"And I'm going with you. No more discussion. We leave tonight." She turned on her heel and went back to the mansion, to her room, and pulled out her gun case.

Suddenly, she sat down, feeling faint. This was all so dreamlike, surreal. She was a wife, and now a widow. Mario was barely in the ground and she had no time to mourn, no time to fall apart. That was a luxury, and she couldn't afford that right now. Later, perhaps, there would be time.

Last night she had barely slept. She had vague memories of Rosa giving her something to help her sleep, but it hadn't worked. She'd tossed and turned all night, thinking of Mario, missing Abby and her mother, wondering what was going to become of them all. And the nightmares . . . full of guns blazing, tunnels collapsing, and screams. So many screams, going on and on and echoing in her head even as the sun rose.

Tonight, she would not sleep again. She was going with Bruno and his men to find those who had killed her husband. Revenge. It was going to be hers.

Jules finished prepping her weapons. Besides the Beretta that she acquired at the campground in Illinois, she was also armed with her wedding present from Mario: a fully automatic AR15. She'd been practicing with it while Mario was gone and was planning to show him how quickly she'd taken to it. Now his enemies would find out firsthand.

She went downstairs, ready to go, and Rosa came in from the kitchen, begging her to stay and let Bruno handle things. News sure travels fast, Jules thought. She shook her head, hugged Rosa, and ran into Father Timothy waiting on the front porch. She sighed.

"Jules, my dear, just where do you think you're going?" asked the priest.

"North," answered Jules, succinctly. In spite of her hurried baptism and her newness to any type of religion whatsoever, it really wasn't in her to argue with a priest. But she would, if pressed. She had no intention of remaining behind, not this time.

It was Father Timothy's turn to sigh. "Jules, I know how you must feel, but the killing has to stop. We should learn to work with these men from the north side."

"Father," said Jules, becoming more and more exasperated. "I'm familiar with the Commandments, especially "Thou shalt not kill," but there comes a time when it's rather necessary. We can 'work with' them when we're in a position of power, and not before. I have no intention of letting Mario's work here be for nothing. And when I get back, I'll sit down and listen to anything you have to say. But not now."

She walked down the steps and to the brewery, to Mario's office, without looking back.

Bruno and those whom he'd selected for this very important mission were waiting. They fell silent upon her arrival and respectfully lowered their heads. Until she stepped behind the desk. Mario's desk.

Jaws dropped; eyebrows were raised. Bruno stood by the door, watching the men's reactions.

"I'm taking over the family," said Jules. "It's what Mario would have wanted."

They all had their doubts about that. They'd known the boss since he was just a boy, and they knew, much better than she could imagine, that Mario would have wanted them to take care of this distasteful business and continue protecting Jules, keeping her safe. Besides, she was young. And a woman.

But none dared argue. They were stricken dumb by her announcement, and she gave them no time to consider the issue as she explained the course of action she had plotted. Of course, she'd discussed this with Bruno, as it was essentially the same thing he'd worked up, with the addition of her presence.

"Let's move out," she told them.

They followed Cherokee until it ended, crossed the rail yards, and stopped on the riverbank - Jules, Bruno, and half a dozen heavily armed men. When they reached the riverbank, Pete was waiting.

Pete had been a boat builder before, and in the years since VADER had created several longboats that the family used to navigate up or downriver. They were simply constructed, wooden, and could carry six rowers, plus a couple passengers and plenty of ammo. Just twenty feet long and barely three feet wide, the boat was crowded with the addition of their supplies; thankfully, it was a short trip.

Gliding under the moonlight, Jules had time to think. She didn't like that. She turned her attention to the shoreline, watching for an optimal place to dock. They passed the remains of the MLK Bridge, the pylons appearing ghostly in the dim light. Jules gave a low whistle and pointed to shore.

They followed Mullanphy Street west, past the old interstate, to Seventeenth Street. It was there, in a former gym, that the north-side gang had their headquarters. Straight into the lion's den.

Jules had decided, and Bruno agreed, that the best way was head-on confrontation. They were going to demand that Mario's killers be turned over to them, and in exchange they would guarantee a truce. If their demand was met, well and good. Those men would be executed. If it wasn't, which was the far more likely scenario, the gang would live to regret their decision.

Jules, followed by Bruno, simply walked to the front door and banged on it with the butt of her rifle. The rest of their had disappeared into the darkness.

The door was yanked open, and bright light illuminated the tall, slender woman and her mountain of a companion. "Who the hell are you?" asked a loud voice.

Jules stepped inside, brushing past the man who'd answered her polite knock. Bruno followed close behind - except Bruno didn't brush past so much as shove the man backwards. They were in a large room, lit by the hum of several generators. They'd obviously interrupted a meeting, and just as obviously weren't expected.

There was a moment of silence and then a whoosh, followed by many clicks, as guns were drawn and leveled at the newcomers.

Jules slowly raised a hand. "We're not here for a gunfight. We are here for my husband's killers."

Laughter exploded around the room, along with a few comments.

"Who that honkey bitch think she is?"

"What the fuck?"

"Hell, I'd tap that, right here, right now!"

"Shut up!" said Jules sharply. "You have one chance, and just one, right now. If those men aren't brought to me within five minutes, I promise that you'll be on the receiving end of a world of hurt."

More laughter. Bruno stiffened, his hands itching to shoot someone. Or many someones.

Jules waited.

"All right, then. You've obviously made your choice." She turned to leave, fully expecting to be hit with a hail of bullets. She walked steadily to the door, Bruno behind her, and held her breath until they were back outside, followed only by more derisive laughter. She could only imagine they'd been allowed to leave simply because they thought she was completely insane.

But they'd bought time - time for the other men to disperse and surround the building with trip wires and mines.

They were halfway back to the riverfront and the waiting boat when the first explosions rose into the sky.

Jules was exhausted. She slept the entire trip back downriver, a small smile on her face.

Robin Tidwell

Chapter Fifteen

They made it as far as the Roosevelt station, where their path was obstructed by rubble. Alison calculated that they were still a dozen blocks from Chinatown. They stopped to consider the next best route to continue out of the city and meet up with Gene at Roseland.

Brad suggested that they go up top, in the air, and split up. Or stay together, but get out of the damn subway. Outside.

Alison told him to suck it up.

While Emmy was fascinated with their exchange, Abby stepped away from all of them and tapped quietly on the monstrous pile of stone that had brought their progress to a halt. She moved a few steps, and tapped again. And again.

"I don't think this is as solid as it looks." She reached into her pack and pulled out a block of C4, looking up at the ceiling. In fact, she strongly suspected that it wasn't a cave-in at all.

"Oh, no," said Brad. "No. You put that in the wrong place and the whole city is liable to come down on us. No, no way!"

"Relax," Abby told him, stifling a grin, "I'm just going to use a little." She crossed the width of the tunnel, looking and tapping, and finally stopped. "This is it."

She carefully packed a small amount of the explosive into several shallow gaps and attached a detonator cord. Humming as she worked, she effectively ignored Brad's protests as Emmy and Alison pulled him back into the shadows and around a bend in the tunnel.

Finishing with the C4, Abby connected the placements with short lengths of detonation cord and left the last one dangling out of the wall. She eyed the distance between the bend around which the others had disappeared. Yes, this could work.

Not quite 300 yards separated them from the explosion; she'd have felt more confident if it was farther, but she was down to the last roll of cord. It would have to do. She hurried to join the others, unrolling the cord as she walked.

She pulled the detonator out of her pack; it looked rather like a staple gun. Connecting the cord, she paused for a second, and pulled the trigger.

WHOOSH!

The explosion itself temporarily deafened them, but the immediate result sucked the oxygen from the tunnel for a split second and rendered them briefly disoriented. Abby was the first to recover, rushing to the blast site. The C4 had done its job and there was a three foot hole blown into the rubble. She shined her light through, and saw nothing beyond but more subway tracks.

The vast majority of the blockage was extremely unstable, and they needed to carefully begin removing rock and debris to increase the size of the opening. It would have to be fast, too. Bits of dust were puffing out from crevices and some loose gravel could be heard hitting the floor.

They worked quickly but carefully, and within twenty minutes were able to boost Alison through the opening, followed by Emmy. Brad was still wondering if they shouldn't go back to the last maintenance door they'd passed, but Abby overrode his protests and shoved him through to the other side as well.

Once they were all together, they made haste down the tracks, going further and further south.

And then suddenly, Jerome appeared around the next bend. And he wasn't alone.

Heavily armed, a group of twenty men were clustered behind him. Abby considered just shooting him for fun, but instead she skidded to a stop, careful to keep her hands in sight and away from her weapons. Alison nearly ran into her. Again.

"Well, well," said Jerome. "And here you are again. I kind of figured you were behind that explosion an hour or so ago. So we came to check it out."

"Hey," said Alison, "It's sonny-boy, back to play in the big leagues!" She grinned and held out a hand. No hard feelings, huh?" Jerome just glared at her. "Fine," she added. "Be that way."

"So, anyway, Larry wants to see you all. Now," he added, trying to sound fierce but falling a little bit short. He motioned to several men, who stepped away from the group and sidled in behind Abby and the others, guns drawn.

They walked for thirty minutes, then went through a maintenance door and descended even further. Abby and Alison knew exactly where this was leading, but Emmy was amazed that there was something below even the subway. Brad, of course, was looking paler by the minute.

Alison squeezed his hand. "Relax. Pretend you're just in a basement or something. You'll get used to it."

"I doubt," he snapped, pulling his hand away. "I think my man card just got revoked."

Alison almost laughed. "Oh, honey, really? Way to be sexist!"

Brad was still grumpy when they reached the large room and entered; Larry was waiting.

"So, we meet again. I trust that this time we can reach an understanding?"

"Depends," Abby told him. "Are Jerome and your goons going to cooperate, or will we have to shoot our way again?"

"Oh," said Larry, with a sigh. "We'll cooperate. It seems we're on the same side and anyway, I don't like being shot at. Or guns, for that matter.

"These youngsters, they don't remember life on the streets back in the old days. That's why there aren't many men my age around these parts. Most of 'em died young."

Abby nodded. She'd heard stories.

Emmy stepped forward. "What do you have in mind?" she asked. "We have a large organization in the area, and our goal is to stop Co-OpCom. If you're good with that, you're with us, and you'll all follow directions.

"That's the offer, and the only one on the table."

Larry nodded. "Just one condition."

"I'm listening."

"When this is over, when the government's gone, you all go on back to wherever you came from and leave us alone. We'll do just fine here in Chicago without any kind of interference."

"Deal," said Emmy, holding out her hand.

Larry took it, they shook, and an almost audible sigh of relief floated around the room.

"Alright," Emmy said, "Tell me what you've got. People, weapons, supplies, all of that."

"This is it," Larry told her. "Twenty men, plus me and my son, Jerome." Abby and Alison exchanged looks. "And his younger brother, Hawk. My wife was taken by the death squads two years ago, and my other boys were killed right after that. The women you met last time you, er, visited us, Jeanine and Marcia, and the two children we rescued. That's it."

"Two?" asked Abby. "There were a dozen here!"

"I know." Larry shook his head. "We did all we could. The others . . . the others just up and died. Wasn't nothing wrong with them that we could see, but . . ."

Abby, alarmed, thought of Elizabeth. And EJ. She hoped they were both okay, and safe, and then she turned her mind back to the here and now. Alison wiped away a tear.

"Go on," said Emmy, remaining stoic and businesslike in spite of her inner grief. "Weapons?"

"They're all right here. We wear what we got, makes it easier to travel around."

"Supplies?"

"Well, we have enough food, I suppose. We had some good raids when it all went down, and since there aren't too many of us, we've managed. Keep supplies comin' in on a regular basis too. And we got some generators, some furnishings. We move around a lot though, mostly aren't ever at our home base."

"And where is that?" asked Emmy.

"Couple blocks south. Right under the police station," said Larry. "'Course, they use it for military police now, and expanded it into a kind of barracks. But we're far enough below and they don't have a clue we're there. We can get there in half an hour or so."

"Nice touch," said Emmy. "Let's go!"

It wasn't a bad setup. They had bunks along the walls in one area for the men, and another for the women and children; a common area, and a storage area. Emmy took Brad and they went with Larry to inventory supplies. She figured it was best to keep Brad occupied and she was right—he finally started to relax a little.

Abby pulled Jeannine and Marcia aside. She wanted to find out all she could about the other children, the ones who didn't survive. The two who were still there looked to be about six years old and were playing quietly in a corner. They didn't look up or show any interest as the women talked.

That left Alison to give Jerome a hard time and she was certainly enjoying herself. But then he asked a pertinent question about her gun and they actually found some common ground. They were deep in a discussion of ballistics when Emmy returned from the storage area.

"Alright," she told them all. "Here's the plan. The four of us are going on to Roseland, plus Jerome—he'll be our runner. I've given Larry instructions, and we'll be formulating plans and meeting up here again in one month."

Abby nodded. She was anxious to get back, not just to Roseland, but to EJ and Elizabeth and to pass along some crucial information to Storm. If it wasn't too late.

After a dinner of canned, room-temperature stew, the five of them, with Jerome leading the way through the tunnels, started out again for Roseland.

They finally surfaced, much to Brad's relief, just south of the Stevenson Expressway, near Mercy Medical. The south side of Chicago had pretty much been left alone, so far, other than the usual semi-destruction. They all knew, however, that it was only a matter of time—and very soon, Co-OpCom would be rounding up those living in the area and moving them north, into the Loop. Or killing them outright.

Ten miles to go, as the crow flies.

Chapter Sixteen

Jules wiped the sweat off her forehead and fought down another wave of nausea. Nearly a month had passed since Mario's murder and it was late September. Not hot enough to make one sick, she mused, unless it was little Frankie, who had been told, over and over, not to eat a sausage that had been left sitting out too long.

She suspected what was wrong, and oh, it was so wrong; she didn't have time for this. But she decided that if she didn't think about it, then it wasn't real. So there.

She washed her face and went in search of Bruno. He had new reports on the north-side gang activity and she wanted to go over them with him. As it turned out, they hadn't eliminated the entire gang, and a new leader had sprung up to take the place of the old.

As Jules heard it, this was the fourth gang leader in as many months. They weren't terribly organized, and not particularly well-armed, but they struck with impunity and under cover of darkness, hit and run, bully tactics. As for their leaders, well, they ended up taking an unfortunate bullet either from Mario's men or their own. They weren't too bright. This new one, she suspected, would be of a similar stripe.

Then she heard the chopper.

Damn.

She looked up, shading her eyes, taking cover. She barely noted the flurry of activity in the street as others did the same. Closer, closer.

The chopper landed and the engines were cut.

Silence.

And Bruno stepped out, followed by a dozen men. Jules blinked in surprise as he walked toward her.

"Okay," said the big man, once they'd reached her office. "So I didn't mention that I flew choppers for the military. Mario knew. Can we move past that now?"

Jules was furious. Bruno had given her a scare that she calculated had taken at least ten years off her life. Not that she was really worried; at nineteen, no one thought about things like that. But she'd read it somewhere and it seemed to fit the situation.

And the situation, as Bruno explained it to her, was that a squad had gone out a couple days ago, scouting far to the south along the Mississippi River. They'd surprised the chopper pilots resting on the ground, summarily executed them, and then sent a runner for Bruno.

"They," he emphasized, "also knew about my former employment."

Jules' anger cooled. A bit. "All right," she said. "Get it under cover and out of sight. Surely they'll come looking for it. Probably sooner rather than later.

"Then we'll talk."

As soon as Bruno disappeared, Jules reached for a trash can under the desk and quietly threw up. Again.

Damn.

Two things to deal with.

"So," she asked Bruno, "what was this chopper doing so far from Chicago?"

Bruno shrugged. "Big Frank said that one of the pilots told him they were just following orders, cruising up and down the river. Yeah, right. How come this is the first one we saw?"

Jules nodded. "Spying?" she wondered aloud. "Or moving up from further south? What's going on down near the Gulf?"

"Nothing, that we know of," answered Bruno. "Not much intel from the southern states. We know that Co-OpCom has Chicago as its headquarters, and there are bases in DC and LA. Maybe Miami. I don't know. You think we should send someone down there?"

Jules thought for a moment. "Yes," she said decisively. "I'll go. Find me three good men, men who are familiar with the country, not just the city boys." She swayed slightly and felt sweat trickle down her armpits.

Bruno studied her carefully for a moment. "Oh, no, you won't. You don't look well, Jules, and you're too important to all of us to risk it, even if you felt better."

"I feel fine!" And then she turned and delicately vomited in the trash can. Again.

"Stay put," Bruno told her. "I'm getting Rosa." He walked out, closing the door, and Jules leaned back in her chair, trying to recover from her last bout of sickness.

Rosa arrived and shooed Bruno from the room. She asked Jules some questions, looked into her eyes and down her throat. Rosa was the closest thing they had to a doctor. She knew all about natural remedies and hoarded what medicines the family possessed. She also presided over gunshot wounds and other injuries and didn't have a squeamish bone in her body.

Rosa stepped back and smiled at Jules shyly. "Un bambino!"

Jules paled. "What? No, no, I'm sure it's something I ate. Or the heat."

"No," said Rosa. "You are going to have a baby. Mario's baby." She clapped her hands together and smiled broadly. "You know this, yes?"

"Yes," said Jules, tiredly. "I knew. I thought I knew." She put her head down and began to cry.

"Oh, bambina, it will be all right," said Rosa, pulling Jules to her feet. She held her and patted her back until Jules stopped crying. "There, see? Much better.

"Now I must tell Bruno." And Rosa opened the office door, calling for Bruno, who came on the run.

"No!" said Jules, as Bruno skidded to a stop in the doorway.

"What?" Bruno asked. "What's going on? What's wrong with Jules?"

Rosa looked at Jules. And then she looked at Bruno. She opened her mouth . . .

"No," said Jules again, sternly

"Yes," said Bruno. "Rosa, tell me what's wrong!"

Jules relented. She could see that Bruno was very upset, and there was no point, really, in waiting. Everyone would know soon. And she knew what that meant as far as her activities were concerned.

"Go ahead," she told Rosa, resignedly.

"Un bambino!" Rosa said joyfully. "We are having a baby!"

Bruno looked at Jules, who was clearly trying to reconcile the idea of having a baby, Mario's baby, and just after his death, too. She also appeared to be trying not to throw up. Again. No wonder she looked sick. He knew nothing about women having babies, but he hoped her symptoms passed soon.

And then he broke into a smile. Babies were cute. Babies were fun. And this would be a special baby, Mario's baby, to continue the family line.

"Cut it out, you two. I get it; I'm having a baby. Mario's baby. But in the meantime, we have things to do. And I don't want anyone else to know, got it?"

Rosa and Bruno sobered up for a moment, but couldn't quite stop smiling. Jules was not amused. She certainly couldn't think of all that this news would entail, not now. Maybe later. Maybe. Holy smoke. A baby. She sat down quickly.

"Come," said Rosa. "You must rest." She grabbed Jules' arm and marched her out the door before Jules could protest. She waved a hand at Bruno. "You take care of things, yes?"

Bruno grinned in response, knowing that as soon as Jules could escape Rosa's clutches, she'd be right back here in the office. He settled into a chair to wait.

It was longer than he expected. When Jules returned, some two hours later, he could tell she felt better. Looked rested, too. Within just a minute, he knew he was right.

"I'm going south, with a squad. That's final."

"No," he told her. "You're not. And that's final. Even if you weren't important to us, your baby is, and no one is going to allow you to take off anywhere."

"No one has to know," Jules argued. "At least not yet."

Bruno laughed. "Do you think Rosa paid the slightest attention when you told us both to keep it quiet? She's already told Angie, probably while you were napping, and Angie's told Teresa and probably Linda and Sharon as well. By tonight, all the men will know." He laughed again.

Jules glared at him. "Fine. But I'm not going to just lie in bed and do nothing but knit booties!"

"Didn't expect you to."

***

They'd reached the safe house in Roseland and had been there for two days. Abby was itching to go back to Joliet and check on EJ and Elizabeth, and Alison offered to go with her. "It'll give Emmy and Brad time to catch up, while they're plotting our next move."

Abby wasn't thrilled to be leaving Emmy so soon. She felt like they'd barely had a chance to talk, and never any time alone. She knew, too, that it was for the good of everyone, and that Emmy was needed here for the time being. So she accepted Alison's offer. It would be good to be on the road again, especially with a partner.

They said their goodbyes and started off as soon as night fell. It was cooler then, especially since they were farther north than they'd been used to, and the moon was bright. Thirty-five miles; about two days, or nights, as it were, if they didn't run into any trouble.

That was a vain hope. Alison's middle name was "trouble."

Chapter Seventeen

Jules coolly eyed the young man standing before her as she slowly circled the pillar to which he was tied. She spoke not a word. Finally, she leaned against the wall and simply stared at him. She pulled out her Ruger and lazily examined it, turning it this way and that.

Sweat began to drip from his brow, and his knees started to shake. Suddenly, she holstered the gun and whipped out her knife. She took two quick strides and stood there, face to face, and watched him begin to silently cry.

"Bruno! Frank!" she called. The two big men threw open the heavy steel door and stood, one on each side of her, glaring at the prisoner.

Now the young man was crying in earnest, unsuccessfully trying to stifle his weak sobs. Jules shrugged and left the room. She had no stomach for torture, but this was necessary. It wouldn't be much. The mere presence of Bruno and Frank was usually enough to crack men older and wiser and more experienced than this one. That, and her own performance.

This one had been caught raiding one of many storerooms scattered about south St. Louis. He'd been alone, surprisingly, as they usually arrived in packs. He'd been brought to Jules on her orders; she needed information. The squad that had gone

127

down the river hadn't yet returned, and she was getting impatient.

They were no closer to finding out what Co-OpCom was planning.

She left the building and went to see George. He'd returned to them a week ago, having been caught in the bombing of the Lincoln Park area in Chicago. He'd briefly rendezvoused with Gene and then hightailed it back to St. Louis. Unfortunately, he'd contracted some type of virus - not VADER, thank heavens - and had deliriously wandered the deserted farmland of Illinois for many days. One of their patrols had discovered him, shivering and nearly starving, over near Cahokia Mounds.

Rosa held a finger to her lips as Jules entered the room where George was recuperating. Damn. Now she'd have to wait for him to wake up. She sighed and sat down, putting up her feet, and motioned Rosa to take a break. The older woman left the room reluctantly. She was worried about all the stress Jules was dealing with, and the coming baby as well.

Jules awoke to George's voice, raspy and low.

"Jules," he said, "good to see you again."

"Good to see you, too," she told him. "Especially conscious and coherent!"

"Yeah, the fever broke last night. Rosa worked her magic again. Tell me what's going on around here. Where's Mario?"

Tears welled up in Jules' eyes. Dammit. She was so emotional these days. "He's dead, George," she said bluntly. "Killed by those cowards up north."

George's face became blank, but his eyes were full of fire. "Who?" he asked quietly. "Who did it?" He struggled to rise, but Jules gently pushed him back down.

"We took care of it, George. Bruno and I, and some of the men. We went up there, to their headquarters, just as soon as we buried Mario."

George relaxed a bit. "How?"

"Why, I knocked on the door," Jules said, with a small smile. "I demanded they turn over Mario's killer, and they laughed. So we left. And set off the detonators."

George was very nearly smiling now. "So what are your plans, Jules? Are you going back to Chicago, to your mother?"

Jules grew tense and her smile faded. "No, George. Mario and I were married. I'm in charge here now." She waited, wondering at George's reaction to her statement.

"Huh," he said. "Well, I'll be." He didn't really seem surprised.

"Now," Jules told him, "I have some questions for you. First, is everyone up there okay? And what happened with the Lincoln Park bombings?"

This time, George managed to sit up a little, as he reached for a glass of water. "It came out of the blue. I was up there with one of Riley's cells. You didn't meet her, but she's the head of the Chicago area resistance. Abby and your mom and Brad are with her." He didn't mention that, at this point, he really didn't know who was where or how they were faring, but he gave her the facts as he knew them.

"Anyway, I was asking questions, getting information, and bam—Co-OpCom was in the sky, raining more hell down on us. I managed to get out and away before it hit the house, but the others had gone downstairs. And it looked like whatever bombs they were using were pretty damn effective. Just a crater in the ground, that's all that was left.

"So I started coming south, and ran into Gene - he's one of us - out scouting for Riley that day. He told me he was pretty sure they had a traitor in the bunch, but he wasn't certain. He was taking that intel to Riley when we camped out that night."

"But why?" asked Jules. "Why were they bombing their own people?"

"Truth be told," said George, "there weren't that many government types up that way. Most of them are down in the Loop, the central downtown district. I imagine they're going to hit the south side of Chicago next, round 'em up and kill 'em all, just like they did here."

"I see," Jules mused. "More than likely they're running out of food and supplies and thinning the herd, so to speak."

"Yep," George answered. "That's what I'm thinking. All those perks they promised everyone, and it's getting harder to deliver, considering how fast they suck up resources."

Jules considered all of this for a few moments, briefly wishing she could be up in Chicago to help whatever plan they had in mind. But no, she knew she couldn't. Her place was here. And anyway, Bruno would throw a fit if she took off. And Frank. And Rosa. All of them.

Except George.

"Jules, if you and I could go up there, it would really be a help to Riley's group, and we could get some better info on what's happening to the south."

Jules jerked her head up and looked warily at George. How did he know about the southern concern?

He reached for her hand. "I talked to Bruno earlier. That's how I know about the choppers moving up from the Gulf.

"And that's why I said 'if.' Congratulations, by the way."

Damn.

"Yes, well," Jules said. "Regardless, I'm still handling things here, just remember that, and I'm ordering you to rest up and get well. We need you here." With that, she gave George a hug and took her leave.

Big Frank met her in the hallway. "Bruno's waiting for you."

The two of them went back to the brewery, to Jules' office.

"Okay," said Bruno, "here's what I've got. The north-side gang has dwindled to fewer than a dozen men. Couple women, too, but they aren't the type to come after us, mostly cowed by their men and pretty much used for just one thing . . ." He glanced at Jules.

"Oh, don't worry about my sensibilities. I can take it." Jules raised an eyebrow. These men just wouldn't learn. She was a lot tougher than they thought, even having seen her in action.

"The kid told me things are pretty rough up there. They don't have a lot of food, the bigger guys take whatever they want from whoever has it, and most of them are pretty tired of it all."

"What are you thinking?" Jules was wary.

"Well," said Bruno, "I'm proposing we let the kid stay. See what happens. Maybe he'll be useful."

"What if he's a plant?"

Bruno shook his head. "I've been doing this a long time, and I don't think so. I think he's just a scared, hungry kid."

"All right," said Jules. "But he's your responsibility. He sticks to you like glue; understood?"

"I'm on it, Jules. I'd never do anything to risk the family."

"I know that, Bruno. And I appreciate your work more than you know." She smiled. "Now, I just talked to George. He thinks, based on what he observed and in talking with members of this Riley person's group, that Co-OpCom is tightening things up. That would dovetail with the choppers being moved up north with only two pilots aboard.

"First, I think they need more firepower and more eyes in the sky. Second, I'm guessing they're closing up some base to the south; probably Miami, as we thought. Have we heard back from Rick and the others?"

"Not yet," Frank spoke up. "Should be close, though. Maybe tonight."

"Let me know the minute they arrive."

"Will do, Jules." Frank inclined his head briefly and left the room.

Bruno hesitated for a moment. "You want I should send a runner to Chicago, Jules?"

She looked startled. "Whatever on earth for? Don't we have enough going on here?"

"Well, um, you know . . ." He shifted uncomfortably.

"Good Lord, no!" She finally got it. "My mother would have a hissy fit and come flying down here to—to—well, I don't know exactly what she'd do, but I don't need to deal with that now. Sheesh."

Bruno left, promising to keep her updated on the "kid," as he kept referring to the newest member of the family.

Jules sat back and rubbed her forehead. Her mother. Alison would trip if she knew what Jules was up to these days. She'd been upset enough when Jules took off for St. Louis. The only way Jules had been able to go was because Abby and Brad were both on her side. If Alison knew that her daughter had gotten married . . . and that Mario was dead . . . And then there was the baby.

Things were different now. When Alison was the same age, she'd been in college and had gotten married right after graduation. She really wasn't much older than Jules was now, and she'd managed fine. Well, fine until her husband disappeared with Jules.

Jules was still conflicted about that. She knew what had happened, she'd lived it, but she'd been so young. Old enough to know something was wrong; too young to know what that was. She had known that woman wasn't really her mother; her mother would have taken care of her. Thank heavens for Grammy. Jules thought of her often. She and Gramps had always taken her in, always made sure she was okay.

And then there was VADER.

Gramps died right before things went crazy. His heart, Grammy had said. And then Jules' dad and that woman had disappeared, and she couldn't find Grammy at all.

And then there was Abby.

Abby took her in, took care of her, taught her how to shoot and how to track. And even though, at just four years old, Jules knew they were constantly in danger, she felt safe with Abby.

Jules still thought about those years at the camp, and after that, when she lived in the cave. And EJ. She really missed EJ, just like a little sister. She missed them all, those who were killed and those still living but far away. But she had a job to do. She couldn't take the time to get all maudlin, and so she roused herself and went out and back to work.

Robin Tidwell

Chapter Eighteen

"What the hell?" whispered Alison as she and Abby ducked into the shadows. "Is that a chopper? Sitting here in a parking lot?"

It was, indeed. And unoccupied, at least at the moment.

"You know how to fly one of these?"

"Nope. You?"

"I wish!" Alison started to move out of the shadows, and Abby grabbed her arm. There were two men, presumably the pilots, walking towards the chopper.

"Stay put," Abby said, "unless it goes downhill. You'll know in a minute." She sidled around the corner of the building with her Mossberg.

Alison clapped her hands over her ears as the shotgun blasted into the air. The pilots did likewise as they slowly turned around to face Abby.

"Ali! Get out here!"

Alison speedily complied, and now the men were covered with three guns. Alison never went just halfway. Two hands, two guns; perfectly logical to her.

"Talk," said Abby. "Who are you, and where are you going?"

Both men remained silent.

"Do you have a death wish, or what?" asked Alison, waving her AR15. She was itching to use it.

"We're flying north," said one of the men, eyeing Alison's weapon.

"To?"

"Chicago."

"Why?"

The man shrugged. "Orders."

"Okay," Alison interjected. "I'm getting awfully tired of these one-word answers. Get to the point!" She walked right up to them and pointed her Sig at the speaker's head. The other one took a tentative step backward.

"Stop," Abby told him, "if you know what's good for you."

Alison almost giggled. "For a second, Ab, I thought you were going to say, 'Stop, or I'll shoot!'"

Abby smiled grimly. "Oh, I will shoot," she told the men. "And this one, she's nuts. I'm surprised you're still alive."

"Hey, no problem! Hang on a minute, and could you put those things away? Someone might get hurt!"

Abby looked at the pilot incredulously. "No kidding? Why do you think we carry them? You Co-opComs are all alike. If guns are good enough for the government, they're good enough for us."

"We're unarmed," said the heretofore silent one. "You can't shoot an unarmed man."

"The hell I can't!" snapped Alison. "Wanna try me? Now, talk!"

"We're just pilots. We're not military. We don't carry guns. We fly troops around, or officials, or - "

"Drop bombs?" asked Abby sarcastically. "But you're 'unarmed?'"

"Well, yeah. But we're just following orders!"

"Yeah. I got that. Now, tell us exactly what these orders entail, or I'm going to blow your brains out." Alison didn't have much patience left - not that she'd had a lot to begin with.

The first one cleared his throat nervously, looking at his companion. The other one nodded, and both of them lowered their hands and reached for pockets on their sleeves.

"Oh, no, you don't!" hollered Alison. "I'm not getting cheated again with one of those suicide pills!" She fired a shot at their feet, and both of them jumped a foot off the ground. "Hand them over or the next shot won't miss. And I'll make sure you die very slowly and very painfully."

The pilots complied, hands shaking. They tripped all over themselves, trying to get the words out and make some sense.

"We came up from Miami."

"Top-secret, there's a whole fleet, but we're all flying separately."

"We're just moving aircraft and supplies."

"But no troops?" asked Abby. "Where are they?"

"Gone."

"Gone?" asked Alison. "Gone where? And when?"

"Well," said the more talkative of the two, "we're not sure. They were there one day; hundreds of them, as usual, patrolling downtown. Then they were gone. The next day someone drove us out to the air base and we flew up here."

The other one nudged his companion. "Tell them the rest."

"Yeah, well, it was weird. No people when we left Miami. Not that we could see. And there wasn't any kind of drill or anything, no reason for anyone to be in the shelters. We were the last chopper out."

Abby and Alison exchanged looks. So there were people down in Miami. But not now. Had they been evacuated? Or run off into the countryside to escape Co-OpCom? But surely not all of them . . .

"Wait a minute," said Abby. "Look at me." She shined her flashlight at their faces. Damn.

VADER was back.

But their own pilots? Strange.

"What was your flight schedule?" Abby asked them.

"We were supposed to be at O'Hare this morning, but we had to put down for a couple minor repairs late this afternoon."

"I see," Abby said. She looked worried.

Alison, who was watching the men carefully in case they tried to pull another suicide stunt, thought she saw a tiny drop of blood appear on the forehead of the man standing closest to her. No, she must have imagined that. He brushed a hand across it and it was gone.

But then another appeared, and another. His buddy didn't seem to notice.

"You know about VADER, right?"

"Well, yeah, it was supposed to kill off all the rebels."

"Yes," said Abby. "And now it's back."

The two men looked at each other, and horror spread across their faces. They dabbed at their faces, but it did no good. Cracks began to appear across their cheeks. They slapped at their arms, their legs. They howled in pain as this newest incarnation of VADER ate away their flesh.

Their screams became moans as they collapsed on the ground, seeming to shrink into themselves as they slowly and inevitably were silenced. And then they were gone.

Alison took a deep breath and said, shakily, "I guess they should have stayed on schedule."

Abby poked the piles of bloody rags with the barrel of the Mossberg. "Well, now we know what happened to Co-OpCom in Miami. At least, those missing people these guys mentioned."

"Yeah," said Alison. "But was it an accident?"

"I don't think so," said Abby quietly. "We need to get to Joliet. We're not far now. It's closer than going back to Roseland, and I want to get EJ. She needs to be with me. We can send Sam back to let Emmy know what's happening."

Alison nodded. "Yeah, let's go. Just one problem." She pointed to the chopper. "What do we do with that?"

***

They walked all night, reaching Joliet by four o'clock, well before sunrise. Things were quiet as they made their way through the deserted city to the old prison. Sam was on guard duty; she never seemed to sleep. She was happy to see them, all in one piece, as it were, and briefed them on the happenings in Joliet the last few days: absolutely nothing.

Abby was relieved and went inside in search of EJ. Yes, she was going to wake up her daughter, and no, she didn't care what anyone thought. Like she ever had.

EJ was so excited to see her mother that she shrieked in surprise. Luckily, the walls were thick, but not enough so that it didn't wake the others. Storm came on the run, and even Elizabeth wandered in, half asleep. Abby was thrilled that Elizabeth seemed to be functioning and even observant, although she showed little emotion and said not a word.

However, Abby kept her attention on EJ and promised to talk to Storm very soon. The older woman took Elizabeth out of the room, and Abby settled in to hear all about EJ's adventures over the last few days.

A short time later, Alison stopped by and gave Abby a thumbs-up. Sam was on her way to Roseland.

Alison took a nap.

Chapter Nineteen

Two and a half days later, they heard a chopper.

Abby grabbed EJ and pulled her along the corridor to the safe room that Sam had prepared weeks ago. Storm was right behind her, dragging Elizabeth, but Alison was still outside. Abby debated whether she should go back out and find her, even if it was against protocol, but at that moment, Alison burst through the door.

"Come outside! It's Gene!"

Of course, Gene would know how to fly this thing. Special Ops and all that. Abby wondered why that hadn't occurred to her; she must be getting old. She rubbed her head and joined the others as they came up the stairs and outside into the prison yard.

They worked quickly to unload the supplies, deciding to use the prison as a base for now. It was virtually impregnable, unlike the house, and would be more likely to survive an air strike. The rest of the group, still quartered in Roseland, was following on foot.

But there was one curious-looking trunk remaining on board.

Early the next morning, the rest of the rebels arrived. Tom immediately disappeared with Emmy, and the others settled into their quarters in the prison. There were a lot of jokes tossed around about cellmates, but everyone got sorted out quickly.

At loose ends until the meeting set for noon, Abby took EJ out for a walk.

EJ chattered for a bit, then became very quiet as they wandered around, still on alert and scanning the sky. It had become a constant way of life for them.

"What's wrong, EJ?"

The little girl shrugged. "Nothing, Mom."

They passed a long-untended home with a massive tangle of weeds out front; it might once have been a garden. EJ stopped and began hunting through the mess; looking for something specific or not, Abby couldn't tell. She waited patiently, both for EJ to finish and to begin talking again.

Finally, EJ stuffed a handful of what looked to Abby like weeds and grass into her pocket and muttered something about showing them to Storm when they got back. Then she got serious.

"Mom, how long are we going to be up here? Are we staying?" A normal enough question for a little girl who'd recently turned nine.

"I don't know, EJ." Abby sighed. She missed her woods and her hills. And Jules was back there, too. But Emmy was here now . . . It was a hard choice. When they first started the journey, all she'd wanted was to find the kids and get them out of wherever they were being held. And, along the way, they'd talked about plans to stop Co-OpCom. Until they arrived, however, they had nothing concrete, no intel to analyze. And then, when they discovered, or were discovered by, locals who were part of the resistance, plans began to materialize.

Abby took her daughter's hand and squeezed it. "I do know, EJ, that it'll be at least a month before I head out of here again. And yes, before you can ask, you'll have to stay here with Storm. But I do need to talk to you about something.

"You remember I told you about Emmy, long ago?"

EJ rolled her eyes. "Yes, Mom. How you were friends since you were little, and went to camp together. And got into trouble."

Abby smiled. "Yes, we did. And I only told you those stories so you wouldn't do the same things! But that's not the point, EJ."

"I know. Mom? Does it still make you sad to think about her?"

Abby bit her lip. This might be difficult for a nine-year-old to process. Heck, it was difficult for her, and she was pushing 50. "EJ . . . Emmy isn't dead."

EJ stopped walking and stared at her mother. "What? How?"

And Abby told her. The PG version, at least.

They walked hand in hand back to the prison.

***

"First," said Emmy, opening the meeting, "Larry is going to send his people out and about in Chicago to see what they can learn about Co-OpCom's plans—both now and in the near future. He'll send a runner as soon as he accumulates enough information, or sooner, if anything major is going down.

"Tom, can you give us a report?"

Tom scratched his head and said, "Damned if I can figure out what they're up to, but I have a few theories. I checked that hazmat trunk from the chopper. It's full of prefilled syringes. Based on what Abby and Alison told us they learned from those pilots, my best guess is that they contain the 'new and improved' version of VADER.

"No way to be certain, of course; we surely can't test it. Best thing is that we have possession of the trunk and they don't. However, it's certainly not enough to inoculate everyone in Chicago, so we have to assume that all the choppers were carrying something similar. Looks like about a thousand doses in there.

"The good news is that all of us appear healthy. Not so much as a sniffle. And I've examined Elizabeth. Far as I can tell, Storm is doing a great job with her, and nothing but rest and continued care are required. She seems more interested and is certainly taking on some self-care, so I'm diagnosing nothing more than selective mutism. She may come out of it; she may not."

Tom sat back down, and Lee rose to update the group on the supply inventory. Sam chimed in with a weapon and ammo count. Then it was Gene's turn.

"Well," he said, "thanks to Abby and Alison, we have a chopper. I can think of a dozen uses for this baby, and the first one is to do some spying of our own up in the city. They likely won't notice us if we avoid the no-fly zones.

"Second idea is to zip on down to St. Louis. I know some of you have people down there and would like to check on them. Now, I'm not proposing a field trip or anything, but I'd like to shoot down there and bring them any news, and vice versa."

Alison was excited about the prospect of finding out what Jules was up to and how she was faring, but she seemed rather nervous about something. She was practically bouncing in her chair when she spoke up. "I have an idea for that chopper."

"Yes?" asked Emmy.

"I'd rather discuss it with you first, if that's okay."

"Sure," said Emmy, shrugging. "So that's it, unless anyone has something to add? Okay, then, we'll have regular daily updates, right here, but other than that, everyone is officially on leave for the time being. Guard duty is posted over on the wall. Be careful, everyone!" She indicated that Alison was to remain as everyone else left the room.

Fifteen minutes later, Alison came out and saw Abby waiting. "I need to talk to you, Ab. Soon. But right now, I'm going to go find Brad so we can have a little 'alone' time." She winked and sauntered off down the hall, humming to herself.

Abby knocked and entered.

Emmy leaned back in her chair and let out a heavy sigh. "These are the times I wish we were back at camp - nothing to worry about except getting bombed to pieces and having enough food. And keeping warm," she added, thinking of the coming winter. It was only early October, but there was starting to be an evening chill in the air.

"I'm amazed, Emmy, I really am. Never thought I'd see 'rebel leader' on your resume!" Abby shook her head. Emmy had certainly put herself out there and done things no one could ever have imagined. Brad had noticed it too, and said as much during the few minutes they'd actually seen each other. Abby spent a great deal of time trying to break through to Elizabeth and helping to organize the upcoming plan, and of course, there was EJ.

But for now, there was Emmy. Still trying to grasp all that had happened to her friend, not to mention that she was, yes, very much alive after all this time, Abby shook her head again. Time. Yes, it would take time to get back to where they'd been. If it ever happened. It made her sad, which was hard to reconcile with the happiness and relief when she first learned that Riley was merely a reincarnation of her old friend.

So. Abby shook off her feelings, messy things, always getting in the way of action, and turned her attention outward.

"Can we take a walk or something? I need to get out of here for a while, get some air. EJ's busy with Storm for the afternoon."

"Sure!" said Emmy, jumping up. "There's a nice park not too far from here, a few trees. There was a lot of damage initially, I guess, but it's all overgrown now."

They went east on Woodruff, dodging trash and debris and fallen utility poles. Less than a mile later, they came to what used to be the Lower Creek Spring Preserve. Several hundred yards into the trees, they reached Spring Creek and stopped.

Emmy sat down and took off her boots, dangling her feet in the shallow water. Abby sat beside her, then stretched out on her back, staring at the sky. It was a beautiful fall day. The leaves were turning, the sky was blue.

"Gene's leaving tomorrow," Emmy said. "He's going to shoot down to St. Louis, give them a heads-up, and check on their progress. If you want to send a note to Jules, you probably should give it to him tonight."

Abby nodded. "And then north, to Chicago?"

"Yes. Just a flyover, to get a handle on activity." Emmy paused. "Did Alison talk to you about this plan of hers?"

"Not yet. What does she have in mind?"

"Assassination. The president. Simple idea, really—cut off the head, the body dies."

"Simple?" asked Abby. "Huh. Leave it to Ali to think that's 'simple.'"

"Well, maybe not the execution, no pun intended, but her plan has its merits. The way Co-OpCom works is that the president has all the power. And I mean all of it. The VP was a figurehead; his so-called advisors are sheep that make announcements written by him."

"He's crossed so many boundaries with his 'proclamations' that I'm surprised no one has made the attempt yet," said Abby.

"He's heavily guarded, all the time. Twenty-four/seven. But here's the plan, and it involves our newly acquired transportation." Emmy lay back on the grass.

"Never mind," said Abby. "I can guess. Alison thinks we should swoop in and take off with him."

"Well, close, yes. Not take off. Execute. In public. Many wouldn't believe he was dead unless they saw it themselves."

"No more TV, video, or news crews." Abby mused. "Might take a while for word to spread."

"Yes," said Emmy, "but it would be all over Chicago immediately, command performance and all that, and Chicago is the key. If it falls, the whole thing collapses."

Abby sighed. "Fine. I'm in. But after that, I'm done. I'm going home." She surprised herself at that statement; she hadn't really thought about it, let alone made a decision. She rolled over on her side, looking directly at Emmy.

They were both silent for some time. Abby wondered what Emmy was thinking about this last comment.

"Yes," said Emmy. "Me too."

Abby was relieved. Maybe things wouldn't ever be the same with Emmy, but this was a start. Right now, there were other priorities. She got to her feet, more slowly than she had back in the old days, and helped Emmy up. They took their time walking back to the prison, companionably silent and lost in thoughts of home.

Robin Tidwell

Chapter Twenty

Jules was glad to see the leaves changing colors along the banks of the Mississippi. Cooler weather was surely on the horizon. It had been a hot and muggy fall so far in St. Louis. She was feeling better now, and the rejuvenation of their part of the city was going well. Some of the men were beginning to set up small shops along Cherokee Street and bartering with each other in their spare time. The shored-up and renovated buildings weren't pretty, but they were functional. Most of the goods had been discovered, long hidden but still usable, in the bombed-out craters around the area.

Everyone had enough to eat, and decent shelter. It was like what Jules had read about the pioneer days. No electric, no utilities, but a small, functional community, working together, trading. Even the gang from up north had been leaving them alone, and Bruno's new assistant was working out well. So far. And since Bruno only ever called him "the kid," everyone else had taken to using that name too. They just called him Kid.

Rosa and the other women were busy making baby clothes and knitting booties. Jules tried, but she just couldn't get the hang of knitting. Much like sewing or other domestic skills, she could if she had to, but she was much more accomplished in other areas.

She gazed at the big map on the wall of her office. All the buildings were marked as to their uses. The new shops and housing were labeled by the proprietors' names. No one actually owned anything; it all belonged to the family. And Jules unquestionably called the shots, with Bruno and Big Frank to back her up.

They'd seen no more choppers, heard nothing from or about Co-OpCom in weeks. Mostly, everyone went about the business of living. Things had been peaceful for a month.

The incoming chopper cut loudly through the walls of the old brewery as Bruno rushed into the office and grabbed Jules, pulling her behind him as they ran down the corridor to the safe room. They waited for Frank to come, to remove Jules from the complex as they'd planned for in just such an emergency.

But it was George who arrived instead. The chopper was friendly, he told them, piloted by Gene from Riley's group in Chicago. They met with him back in the conference room. Jules' legs were shaking. This had been not only a wake-up call for the precariousness of their situation, a sign to remain vigilant, but, for the first time, the baby became real to her - a real person, not just a condition that often kept her from doing as she pleased.

She settled into her chair, bringing her mind into focus but resting her hand on her stomach as expectant mothers everywhere have done. None of the men noticed.

If Gene was surprised when the three big men deferred to Jules, he didn't show it. He'd been told upon his arrival of Mario's death, and he offered Jules his condolences, as well as letters from Abby and Alison. He was impressed with what he'd seen so far of their rebuilding and was anxious to learn of any new information.

In answer to his question, Jules frowned. "No, there was no trunk on board our chopper. Just supplies, much as you described. And no pilot suicide either." She glanced at Frank.

"So you think they've abandoned Miami and are concentrating on Chicago alone?"

Gene nodded. "And if something isn't useful, it's going by the wayside. Like people. We think they're losing their grip on the general population and are planning to hang on to only Chicago until they can regroup. If they can."

"That," said Jules, " would explain why they've left us alone for a couple months. They're simply busy elsewhere and are running out of resources to make us compliant. George, would it be possible for you and Gene to fly down to Miami? I think that would be the best place to start. We can find out if Gene's pilots were telling the truth, or at least minimize the uncertainty."

"That's exactly what I was hoping for," said George. "Between the two of us, we can fly down and back within 36 hours, maybe even have some time to go over a few places between here and there."

"What about fuel?" asked Jules.

Gene waved a hand dismissively. "Those Co-OpCom pilots had some on board, which we left in place, plus the overly large tanks themselves. And I'm sure, if we need to, we'll be able to spot where they stopped too. Nothing between here and there except what they controlled, so it won't be hidden."

Bruno spoke up. "What about any rebels down in those parts? No one has come up this way in years, if ever, but surely there are groups down south too. Better take a couple extra men, and a stock of ammo, just in case." He turned to Jules. "I'd like to go, if that's all right."

Jules nodded, deep in thought, and she missed the look Bruno and Frank exchanged. Big Frank knew it was on him alone to protect Jules for the next few days. He'd stick to her like glue.

"I think I'll take the kid, too. Be good for him to get away for a few days, see how real men operate. Those women are coddling him too much."

Jules agreed. Rosa in particular treated Kid like a ten-year-old instead of a teenager. "Fine," she said. "You'll leave in the morning. Now, Gene, if you'll come with me, I'll show you all we've done here in the last year." She rose, as did the men, and walked outside. Frank followed them, at a distance, and George and Bruno went to pack.

Strolling down Cherokee, Jules pointed out the shops and explained their bartering system. Sometimes it involved goods, sometimes services. Just then, Rosa hurried out of the nearest doorway and stopped them.

"Jules, look! Marco found some sweet little baby blankets in a house over on Pestalozzi!"

Jules was furious but tried to remain calm. "I'm sure they will be perfectly fine for your daughter, Rosa. Gene, let's go. I want you to meet Father Timothy." She began pulling him along, chattering like mad, leaving a bewildered Rosa standing in the street.

"So, Rosa's daughter is going to have a baby soon, and that's all Rosa can talk about. All the time. Oh, look, there's Father now!" Jules waved, but Gene lowered her arm and turned her to face him.

"Jules. Rosa doesn't have a daughter, does she?"

Tears came to Jules' eyes. "No," she whispered.

"And she's talking about your baby, isn't she?"

"Yes."

Gene threw up his hands. "Jules, honey, I know we just met and all, but I know your mother pretty well, and I know she's worried about you. Not that she ever talks about it much, but you should have seen her face when she handed me the letter for you.

"She doesn't know about Mario, or that you're running the show down here, and now there's a baby? Good Lord, what am I going to tell her when I get back?"

Jules had gotten a grip on her tears, and she snapped, "Nothing! Tell her I'm fine, I'm well, I'm doing some real work down here. I suppose you have to tell her about Mario . . . but please, please don't mention the baby! She'll want to come down here and—and -"

"Relax, little girl, I guess I can keep quiet about the baby. For now. At any rate, I can tell you there are big things about to happen in Chicago, and your mom is involved to the hilt. She's not leaving for a while, another month at least. Heck, they couldn't do without her at this point."

Jules began to calm down. She even smiled a bit. Yes, that sounded like Alison. Crazy schemes; lots of shooting, naturally. Big guns. And a little tequila. Which reminded her.

"I do have something for you to take back to my mom, and Abby and EJ. But promise me, Gene, that you won't mention the baby?"

Gene nodded, reluctantly.

"All right then, come on. I really do want you to meet Father Timothy. And then I'll show you the homes we've fixed up, the ones that weren't hit too badly in the bombings."

Gene followed her, shaking his head and wondering what the world had come to when a young girl like Jules was the head of an organized group of rebels, as well as a widow and a soon-to-be mother.

The chopper left early the next morning, going south to Florida. Gene took the controls, with George as his co-pilot and Bruno and Kid and three others in the back. None of them had flown before, and by the time they touched down near Nashville, they all looked a little green.

They got out, those in the back a little more hastily than their pilots, and stretched their legs. There were no people in sight, but they weren't expecting to see any. When VADER was released, most of the survivors seemed to have been clustered in the cities. And later, well . . . Colonel Barton wasn't the only petty bureaucrat who was given orders to destroy most of the countryside.

Sure, there were probably pockets of survivors scattered here and there, but that's how they'd survived in the first place: by hiding. At this point, if any had managed to live this long, they probably were doing just fine on their own and not anxious to have contact with anyone—especially anyone who might be the government.

Back in the air, with George at the controls, Bruno moved forward to watch and learn. He was curious about the workings of the chopper, and George was happy to show him. It would certainly help to have a second pilot in St. Louis.

They set down again near Atlanta, far from the city limits. They needn't have bothered. This once- bustling southern hub was nothing more than overgrown ashes and heaps of concrete. They didn't stay long.

It was nearly midnight when they reached the southern tip of Florida. Gene circled the area, using the powerful spotlight attached to the undercarriage. No one was shooting at them; no choppers rose to greet them. They bivouacked in a precariously leaning shed that seemed to have avoided a direct hit and waited for sunrise.

It was just as the Chicago pilots had said. Gone. Miami International was a graveyard of planes and trucks and a few cars. The terminals were demolished. It was eerily silent. They flew east toward Miami Beach, circling back over the peninsula. No movement on the ground except trash and debris disturbed by the rotors of the chopper. Piles of rubble. Gone.

George pointed the chopper north. Nothing left to see here.

They arrived in St. Louis in the late evening. Gene was anxious to go back to Joliet and declined to wait until morning. He'd slept a good deal of the way back, with George at the controls and Bruno acting as co-pilot. Besides, it was just a three-hour flight.

He took with him a note from Jules to Alison, along with a bottle of tequila, and a new knife sheath for Abby. He also had a supply of books for EJ. He'd told Jules about EJ's interest in plants and healing, and somehow, somewhere, Jules had found these.

And just before he left, he leaned down and whispered dramatically to her, "Don't worry, your secret's safe with me!" Jules was still giggling, mostly in relief, when the chopper lifted off.

Robin Tidwell

Chapter Twenty-One

Much of Abby's time was spent with Elizabeth, sitting in silence. She knew the girl had been through some horrific event, and though there was nothing physically wrong with her, she would not speak or even gesture. Storm was hopeful that time would heal her, but Abby wasn't so optimistic. Then again, it hadn't been more than a few weeks since she'd been rescued.

There had been talk among the tunnel people as to what had occurred on the top floors of the Contemporaine. None of the children held prisoner there had exhibited Elizabeth's symptoms, but some had died of unknown causes. Abby suspected the new incarnation of VADER, as the children had been taken to be experimented upon, but perhaps there was more to the situation than any of them knew.

And, too, there was Johnny. Once or twice, Abby had asked Elizabeth about Johnny, but the abject look of terror on her face had ended the topic immediately. Johnny, when he had first come to live with them and Walt and the others, had also remained silent, out of choice. That had been attributed to the deaths of his parents, which he had witnessed. Many mental issues ran in families, so Elizabeth's mutism wasn't entirely out of the norm for her, but something had to have triggered it. She'd been so strong and so feisty prior to her abduction.

Knowing Emmy's story, Abby feared the worst.

She spent as much time as she could with EJ. They went out in the country and practiced tracking. Abby helped EJ perfect her aim with the Glock and taught her how to use other firearms from their well-stocked arsenal. Several times, EJ would tag along with Alison and Brad and learn both defensive and offensive maneuvers. Always, she'd come back with Brad as her prisoner. It was hard to say whether he was allowing her small victories or if she really was that good.

She really was that good.

One day, EJ wandered off alone. She wasn't supposed to do this, but decided to slip out when everyone was busy doing something else. She walked through the neighborhood near the prison, looking for certain plants that Storm had been wanting. Then she saw him.

She hunkered down in the weeds and remained very still. She had her knife, a smaller version of Abby's, and she had her Glock. The man came closer and closer, looking about warily, but taking no real precautions to avoid detection. EJ had never seen him before. He was tall and thin and seemed very nervous. But still, he kept coming closer.

EJ held her breath. He'd stopped right next to her, less than three feet away. EJ let out all her pent-up breath in one loud shriek and tackled him behind the knees. He went down with a thud. In a flash, she had her knife out and at his throat as she straddled his legs. She grabbed the whistle that Sam had given her and blew as hard as she could.

Abby and Emmy came on the run, but skidded to a stop at the unlikely scene. They could barely contain their laughter as they helped Jerome off the ground. He was quite shaken and thoroughly embarrassed to have been taken down by a kid. A girl.

Abby took Jerome back to the prison yard, and Emmy followed with EJ.

"You did a great job back there, EJ. It could have been anyone besides Jerome, and probably not one of us. But you really shouldn't wander around by yourself anymore."

EJ was suddenly shy. Here was Emmy, who she'd heard stories about all her life, and she was real. And not dead. And this was the first time she'd been alone with Emmy since her mom had told her that Riley was really Emmy. EJ wasn't confused or anything, but she had lots of questions and couldn't decide where to start.

Emmy wasn't sure what to say either. When George had told her about Abby and EJ, she'd been surprised that there was a child, but not shocked. She'd known all about Noah's feelings for Abby, so long ago. In many ways, EJ reminded her of Abby as a child, but not entirely; there was a lot of her father there too. But at this point, she didn't know what her relationship was to EJ, or if there would be one at all after they succeeded in taking down Co-OpCom.

If they were successful. But, no. When. It had to be when, or there was no point in . . . well, in anything.

Much like Abby fifteen years ago when she found Jules, Emmy didn't have a lot of one-on-one experience with children. But this was Abby's daughter. She'd do her best. And Emmy's best was always very, very good.

"EJ," said Emmy. "I'm your mom's friend, and I'd like to be yours too. I know she told you about me, not just back when we were kids together, but recently - the last few years or so. Anything you need, if you can't find your mom, you come to me. I wasn't there for either of you for a long time, but I will be now.

"And I'm not going to say any more, because I might cry, and I can't have everyone seeing me like that! But you're an awesome kid. Your mom did a fantastic job." Emmy dabbed at her eyes a bit, turning her head away.

"So, we're back and I've got work to do. See you around, kiddo!" And Emmy hurried inside.

EJ was thoughtful the rest of the afternoon, wondering about all the questions she wanted to ask her mom and Emmy.

Jerome hadn't just been wandering. He brought news: the president was scheduled to arrive in Chicago in three weeks. It was time to act.

As soon as Gene arrived from St. Louis, Emmy called them all together.

"This," she told them all, "is going to be my last mission. If we succeed, I'll be going home, to Missouri. I want my life back, my old life. Any of you are welcome to join me." She held up a hand at their protests, and when the room got quiet again, she continued.

"You've known me only as Riley: a commander, a leader. You learned about my past with Co-OpCom, and you stuck with me. I am grateful for that, as well as the trust you've placed in me all along. But this isn't me. I left my life back home, and that's where I'll go when this is over.

"If we don't succeed, there will be no going back, for anyone, ever. And more than likely, we'll all be dead.

"Now, we have two weeks to get ready. First, Lee, I want you to divide the supplies. I have a detailed list, but we need to know numbers—who wishes to remain in the Chicago area, who will go to St. Louis, and who may want to go elsewhere. Supplies will be divided accordingly."

No one said a word, and they all looked soberly around the room at each other.

Alison raised an eyebrow. "Good heavens, we're not at a funeral. Yet. I know Abby's going with Emmy, and Brad and I are with them. EJ and Elizabeth too. Now, make a decision already, folks. Time's a-wastin'."

One by one, each of them spoke up.

Tom elected to remain in the area, with Lee. Bart and Dave planned to go west, out to the middle of nowhere, as Bart put it, and get away from everyone, no offense, present company excluded. Storm decided to go with the others to Missouri to help care for poor Elizabeth as long her services were needed. Gene planned, for now, to be based in Chicago and help out as needed, but also to act as a liaison between the two cities. And Sam was going with Emmy.

"Okay, it's settled," said Emmy. "And please do remember, this isn't set in stone. And, if all goes well, we'll certainly be free to move around the country anywhere we wish. Well, like we do now, but without worrying about being blown up!

"Jerome has been given leave to speak for his people. They will remain in Chicago, in the city, and attempt to rebuild. We might," she added, glancing at Gene, "want to send them some help from St. Louis. From your report, they appear to have it well in hand."

Gene nodded. "Mario started the renovations, and Jules is quite competent at carrying on his legacy. Perhaps some of her men could make the trip, after the dust settles."

Alison was still stunned at the turn of events in her daughter's life. She couldn't wait to see her again, especially having read the note Jules had sent back with Gene. And the tequila was a nice touch too, she thought, smiling. But really, Jules at the head of a large group, a "family," as Gene said? She jumped when she heard her name, and Abby nudged her in the ribs.

"Um, yeah. What?" asked Alison.

Emmy rolled her eyes. "It's your turn. Tell everyone about this plan you concocted."

"Oh. That." Alison jumped up and walked to the front of the room. "It's simple, really, and based on what I know from my time with Co-OpCom. Knew that would come in handy. So, anyway, this is what we're going to do."

When she finished, several stared at her as though she'd completely lost her marbles. A couple of them nodded thoughtfully. Abby just grinned. Alison really was the best at scheming.

Chapter Twenty-Two

Emmy met with Tom after everyone else left to attend to their assignments. "Is there anything we can do about this new strain of VADER?" she asked him.

Tom shook his head. "I don't know. I'd say destroy it, but the first question is how, and the second is why bother? I mean, we've already assumed this isn't the only batch. Might be a drop in the bucket compared to their stockpiles. If we could get rid of it, that would save, what? A thousand people? How many you figure are in the Chicago area right now?"

Emmy quickly ran some figures through her head. "Let's see. We lost almost everyone with the initial outbreak; then again, in this area, probably fewer than in some others. I'd guess we started here with around half a million, after VADER and before the roundup into the city itself.

"Lost a lot of people to other illnesses, rioting, lack of supplies, general accidents . . . birthrate is practically nonexistent. I'd have to say around twenty thousand here now, or fewer. Of course, that includes top officials, and those who are on our side."

"Hmmm. Between the president and his cabinet, their bodyguards, troops, support personnel, that might account for a few thousand," said Tom, "so that still leaves probably 10K.

"I think we have to bet on there being more of these trunks out there. A lot of them. Doesn't seem to matter to Co-OpCom how many they kill—look at what happened in Miami. And if our theory is correct, LA and DC are probably long gone."

"We can't spare Gene to go to either coast right now. He's going to be busy flying back and forth to St. Louis for the time being, and locally too. So, if we could find these other trunks, how could we dispose of them?" asked Emmy.

"I don't know. It's going to take some time to analyze the components and try to learn how it's spread and who's affected. I'd like to set up down in the rec room here and get to work, but I'm afraid I won't be much use to you in the meantime. I'll have to quarantine myself, just in case, and we darn sure don't want to expose anyone else."

BOOM!

"Crap," said Emmy. "They're at it again. Should we revise our figures?" She ran out the door, Tom right behind her. The noise was far enough in the distance that she knew the bombs weren't falling here. She shaded her eyes and looked to the northeast. Yes. South side of Chicago. Damn. She hoped Larry and his people were safely underground while this was going on. They were a key part of Alison's plan.

"Well, we knew it was coming," said Tom. "So, am I right, you're going to look for the rest of those trunks?"

"Yes. At the very least, we can remove them from, er, present ownership and relocate them. Get to work on this, Tom. It's important. You know how much. Keep me posted."

Emmy caught up to Abby just as she was coming out of Elizabeth's room. "Can we talk?"

The two walked outside and into the old prison yard. "What's up?" asked Abby.

"Couple things," said Emmy. "First, I need your help with a special project. And Brad and Alison too. I know Brad's been kind of at loose ends, and Alison's crazy enough that I'm sure she'll jump on this.

"Second, I want to send EJ and Elizabeth, with Storm, down to St. Louis. They'll be a lot safer there than here."

Abby nodded. "I was thinking the same thing. Much as I hate for EJ to be so far away, this is going to be really bad - one way or another. Storm can take care of them both, and Jules is there. Gene said they're making a lot of progress."

"All right," said Emmy. "Gene can fly them down whenever they're ready. Now, about this project. I want to find those trunks and get rid of them."

"How?" asked Abby.

"I'm still working on the details," Emmy admitted, "and Tom's working on the disposal part. He's setting up his lab down in the old rec room to try to figure out what this new batch is made of and how it works. We know what it does, for sure, but we don't know if it spreads the same way or affects the same types of people. I'm hoping he can find out.

"At any rate, this could be dangerous. I mean, more so than our usual activities."

"Yeah, I get that," said Abby. She shrugged. In for a penny, in for a pound. At least EJ would be safe. "Okay. When does Gene leave?"

"Tomorrow morning."

Tomorrow came way too soon for Abby. She buckled EJ into the chopper, spoke a few quiet words to Elizabeth, and hugged Storm. The older woman smiled briefly and inclined her head. Abby knew EJ would be safe with her. She kissed her daughter one more time, and stepped back. The chopper rose and banked, flying south.

Jules shaded her eyes as the chopper came in for a landing. They weren't expecting Gene back so soon, but she could tell by the markings that it was from the Chicago group. The first to climb out was a woman that Jules didn't recognize, and then a young teenager. And last, there was EJ.

Jules ran to her and swooped her up in a big hug, no mean feat considering how tall EJ had grown in the last few months and Jules' advancing pregnancy.

"EJ! I can't believe it!" Jules turned to Gene. "What's happening up there anyway?" She knew it must be pretty serious if Abby had sent EJ away.

"All in good time," Gene told her, raising a brow. "This is Storm; she's part of our group up north. She's a healer, a good one. And, Jules—you surely remember Elizabeth?"

Jules turned to the silent girl. "Elizabeth?" She looked questioningly at Gene as she noted the slack expression on the teen's face. Jules never would have recognized her, she looked so - so blank. And of course, it had been almost a year. Jules knew that she, herself, had changed quite a bit in that time. She smiled and took Elizabeth's hand.

"I'm glad you're here. All of you," she added, looking around at the group. "Come, let's get you settled in. Gene, I'll see you shortly, yes?"

The pilot nodded. "I'll be waiting."

Jules led the little band of refugees to the house on Lemp Avenue. She found Rosa, who rallied the other women, and within a very short time Storm and Elizabeth were set up in a room together. EJ was going to stay with Jules.

"EJ, I have to go over to the brewery and talk to Gene. I'll be back shortly and we'll have lunch with everyone. Storm is next door, and Rosa and Jeanine will be here. Stay in the house, okay? I won't be long."

"I'm sorry about Mario," EJ said sadly. "I liked him."

Jules stopped in her tracks. She was becoming used to his absence and thought she had moved beyond condolences, but EJ's statement stunned her. She turned and looked at EJ.

"I do, too, honey." She hugged the little girl and tugged on her braid. "I'll be back in a bit."

Gene was waiting in her office.

"Okay, spill, what's going on up there?" Jules demanded.

"Relax," said Gene, "it's not that bad. Emmy's got some plan to find the rest of those trunks, and she and your mom and Brad are going to get them away from Co-OpCom. And then they're going after the president. Abby just wanted EJ and all of them down here, away from any fallout.

"Elizabeth has been . . . different, since the rescue. She won't speak - at all. She's compliant, won't cause any trouble, and Storm has been taking care of her. She's come a long way, but, well... She's not capable of much."

"What was in that trunk?" asked Jules, getting to the important stuff first.

"VADER."

"VADER?!" she shouted. "Again? Crap."

"Yeah," said Gene. "Crap. And a whole host of other descriptive terms. But best we can figure out, the government's using it on their own people, reducing the numbers, so to speak, to conserve resources. Hell of a thing, but that's how they operate.

"So the idea is to get the syringes, hide them, destroy them, whatever it takes. Our doc, Tom, is working on the how-to for that part of the plan. But Emmy and the others, they've got to find the supply first."

Jules sat down and rubbed her head. But . . .

"Wait a minute," she said slowly. "Did you say 'Emmy?' Not—no. Emmy? That Emmy? Not possible!"

Gene looked startled. "Did you know Emmy?"

Jules couldn't answer. She was trying to catch her breath, to stop the tears. Her hands were shaking. Emmy?

She remembered trips to the lake with Abby and Emmy; Emmy teaching her how to tie knots and make a bedroll; Emmy helping with her lessons and tucking her into bed at night. And the last time she saw Emmy, as Abby carried her up the hill and away from the destruction of the old infirmary, Emmy screaming at Abby to run, to take Jules, to run . . . BOOM!

Jules swallowed, hard. She took a deep breath. She gripped the arms of the chair.

"Yes. I knew Emmy."

Chapter Twenty-Three

When Jules got back to the house, the place was in an uproar. Now what? she thought. Really, how many shocks was one supposed to manage in a single day? She was still reeling over the fact that Emmy was alive and well and had once been known as Riley. Gene had filled in the details for her; and while she was still a bit skeptical, she was truly overwhelmed by the news. Emmy? She shook her head and went inside to see what else was happening on this crazy day.

The cause of the chaos was Elizabeth. Elizabeth, who'd only spoken Abby's name a handful of times since she'd been rescued from the clutches of Co-OpCom. Sweet, compliant Elizabeth was screaming her head off, and no one had been able to soothe her for more than a few minutes at a time. Jules stuck her head in the room, and the girl was immediately silent.

EJ was sitting on the bed, hands over her ears; Rosa and Jeanine were wringing their hands and muttering. Storm arrived on Jules' heels with a cup of tea.

"What in the world?" asked Jules.

The teenager turned to face her. "Juliet?" And then Elizabeth burst into tears and sank down into sofa, head in her hands.

Jules took the teacup from Storm and shooed everyone from the room. She sat down next to Elizabeth and put her arms around her, holding her until the tears finally stopped.

"Elizabeth. You know who I am?"

"Yes."

"Do you know where you are?"

"Yes. St. Louis."

"Good." Jules was stumped. Now what was she supposed to do? She tried to remember how much, if anything, she'd read over the years about mental issues. She had vague memories of Cal's last few weeks, the stress and strain of the years in hiding accumulating so much as to become unbearable. Abby had never talked about it. Jules knew that Cal had finally shot herself when the choppers came the last time, but she hadn't seen it, and she really hadn't paid much attention to the problems they were dealing with. She'd only been eight, younger than EJ was now.

"Do you want to talk about it?" asked Jules, hesitantly.

Elizabeth shook her head.

Jules sighed. Was she going back to the silent routine again? Gene said it had been going on for months already.

"I can't," said Elizabeth. "Not now, maybe not ever. But I'm tired of just existing, I'm tired of thinking about . . . everything. I want it to stop."

"Um, what is it you want to stop?" Jules asked uneasily, thinking of Cal again.

"The thinking. It just plays over and over in my head, and I can't change it and I want it to stop. I want to live, not just sit here anymore." Tears crept down Elizabeth's cheeks, but she wasn't sobbing; she only looked incredibly sad. "Will you help me, Juliet?"

"Yes, of course," said Jules, hugging her. "Absolutely."

Jules called for EJ first, who stepped tentatively into the room, looking nervously at Elizabeth.

"EJ," said Elizabeth. "It's okay. I'm back now." She held out her hands. EJ walked over to the sofa and glanced at Jules, who nodded.

"Wow, that's great, Elizabeth! We were all so worried about you, Mom especially. She came and sat with you every day."

"I know," said Elizabeth, "and I'm sorry I caused so much trouble. I knew she was there; I just didn't want to talk. I couldn't talk. I was afraid someone would ask me about . . . about stuff that happened. And I still don't want to talk about it. I don't, I don't!" She began to cry again.

"It's okay, honey," Jules told her, taking her hand. "EJ and I, we understand, right?"

EJ nodded and took hold of Elizabeth's other hand. "She's right. You don't have to tell us anything that you don't want to. You can just start over, like the girl did in that book I just finished, 'The American Queen.'"

Elizabeth showed the ghost of a smile. "I wouldn't mind being a queen."

"Not all it's cracked up to be," Jules muttered. If she didn't stand up for herself, Rosa would have her lying in bed, being waited on hand and foot and knitting booties. "Never mind. EJ, will you go out and get Storm? I think she needs to come meet our Elizabeth."

***

By evening, Jules was exhausted. She'd learned about Emmy; dealt with Elizabeth; seen the chopper off after lunch, as Gene insisted he had to return immediately; and had a long conversation with Bruno about some new activity to the north.

Big Frank and Kid had brought a twin bed into Jules' room for EJ, and the two girls settled down for the night. Jules yawned as EJ started chattering about this and that, and life in Chicago, and fell asleep within seconds.

She awoke with the sun, as well as with EJ's face inches from hers, and immediately jumped up. "What?"

"Nothing," said EJ. "I was worried. You conked out so fast last night, and I had so much to tell you!"

Jules stretched and yawned. "Well, I have a few things to tell you, too. Come on, let's go find some breakfast. I'm starving!"

EJ and Jules wandered around the area all morning, Jules pointing out the sights, as it were, and introducing EJ to everyone. She'd told George to handle whatever came up, and announced that she'd be busy elsewhere for most of the day.

Late afternoon found them on the banks of the Mississippi, staring up at the clouds.

"Jules? When are you going to tell me about the baby?"

Jules sat up with a start. "How the heck did you know? You're just a little kid!"

"No, I'm not," said EJ, stubbornly. "Besides, anyone could tell at this point. You just . . . you know."

"Know what?" Jules snapped.

"Nothing," muttered EJ. "Never mind."

"Come on," said Jules. "It's nearly time to go back anyway. And no, before you can ask, I'm not mad. Just a little sad."

EJ took her hand, and they walked back to the house.

For the next few weeks, Jules spent a lot of time with EJ and Elizabeth. The latter had recovered, and, while still shy around the men and even sometimes with Rosa and Jeanine, she began to resemble the girl who'd been taken away almost two years ago.

Storm had immediately found her place in the household, and she traded secrets and remedies with the other two women. They could often be found together, discussing the impending childbirth and guessing at the sex of the baby.

For Jules' part, she was resigned that this was happening. After all, there was nothing she could do to stop it, and besides—this was Mario's baby. Her love, gone too soon and so quickly. She alternated between periods of deep sadness and boiling rage. She blamed the mood swings on her pregnancy.

And then Bruno brought her an urgent message.

In some ways, she was relieved. She'd gotten caught by Rosa and Jeanine and was at the center of a discussion about appropriate behavior for someone "in your condition." She was about to blow a gasket when Bruno arrived. Pleading work, she made her escape.

When she got to her office, George was pacing. Big Frank lounged against a wall, and Kid was nowhere in sight. Bruno had stuck to her like glue on the short walk over, hand on his revolver, so of course she knew something was up.

"Where's Kid?" she asked.

Bruno smiled. "You didn't see him? Good. He is learning."

Jules rolled her eyes at him. "Really? You're using me for practice?"

"Who better?" said Bruno. "Get used to it. He'll be shadowing you from here on out. George?"

"Yes," said George. "We've had word of activity to the north. Rumor has it that you're the target, Jules."

She sighed. You'd think those guys would have better things to do than chase after a pregnant woman, even if she did happen to be the leader of their biggest rivals.

"What is their problem, anyway?" she asked. "Surely they can see that all we're doing here is a good thing, and they could do it too if they'd just stop being a bunch of posers.

"Well, anyway, it'll take forever for them to get organized to actually do anything, so it's probably nothing to worry about anyway."

"Jules," George said gently, "sit down, please."

She did.

"Jules, they got to Father Timothy last night. They left you a message."

"What? What happened? Is he okay?" Jules jumped up to go see for herself, but Bruno grabbed her arm.

"No, Jules. There is nothing you can do for him." Bruno crossed himself and lowered his head.

Jules sunk back into the chair, hands folded but sitting ramrod straight, and her voice was icy. "What was the message?"

George unfolded a bloodied piece of paper. "'Give us the bitch or you all die. She dies anyway.' It was nailed to his face, Jules. He was still alive when we found him, for just a few minutes."

She stared at the piece of paper, still in George's hands. The room began to dim, she saw flecks of white float across her vision, and then . . . nothing.

Chapter Twenty-Four

"I'm betting on Midway," said Emmy. "If I'm wrong, we'll go up to O'Hare next. But it looks to me like there's a whole fleet of choppers here." She handed the field glasses to Abby. "What do you think?"

Abby focused in on the area to which Emmy pointed her. "Yes, I think you're right." She handed the glasses back and adjusted her shoulder holster, checked her knife. She nudged Alison. "Ready?"

Alison nodded and touched Brad's shoulder. All four jumped up and dashed across the open space near the corner of Central Avenue and 63rd Street. They ducked into the tiny booth that was once space for one or two parking attendants. It was a bit crowded.

"Now what?" asked Brad. There was a maze of runways between them and the targeted fleet.

"Just a second," Emmy said as she peered through the glasses, scanning left and right. "No movement. Let's go!"

They rushed out of the building, ran across at least six runways, and stopped at another tiny structure. Unfortunately, this one was manned, albeit a bit larger. Much larger once the sole occupant had been eliminated. Brad muttered something unintelligible as he dragged the body outside. He and Emmy took up opposite positions to watch for interference, and Abby

175

and Alison crept out the door and over to the grounded aircraft.

The choppers' doors were either missing or unlocked and it was quite simple to do a quick check for any familiar trunks or cases that would likely contain more syringes filled with VADER. They located what they could only assume were the right ones, heavily padlocked. Twenty in all.

A mad dash back to the shed-like structure, and Emmy gave the signal. They waited just minutes for Gene to land. All four of them joined him on the tarmac and, working as teams of two, began transferring trunks from the grounded choppers to their own.

They worked efficiently, but did not rush. If anyone came across the field toward them, they were prepared to either lie or shoot their way out of the situation. They appeared to any casual observer to be part of Co-OpCom, pilots or technicians, thanks to a supply of uniforms the group had acquired over the years.

Naturally, just before the last two choppers were to be emptied, a young lieutenant strolled around the corner. He jumped to attention when he saw Alison and saluted. "Captain!"

Alison glared at him. "What are you doing out here, soldier? This is a top-secret operation. No one is allowed in the area."

"Y-yes, sir. Ma'am. Sorry, ma'am!" The kid was so green he was shaking. He wasn't sure now if he was supposed to salute, or walk away, or even turn his back on this "captain," and so he just stood there, gaping.

"What's the matter with you?" Alison demanded. "Go on, get out of here! And if you breathe a word of this, I'll shoot you myself!" The kid turned and ran like the hounds of hell were on his tail.

The foursome loaded the last trunk, and Gene lifted off. Safe. For now.

***

Tom came up from his basement lab to address the group. He looked as though he hadn't slept in days, and his normally thin frame was even more gaunt. He ran a hand through his hair and sat down wearily.

"I've run all the tests that I can possibly come up with, and I can tell you that this is a virus that will take down just about anyone. The difference is that it's not targeted, like the original VADER, even though that one didn't work so well. I suspect this one is even more potent.

"The good news is that this, too, is likely spread only by direct injection. Likely. The bad news is that even though we were all immune to the first one, we may not be to this one."

"What about disposal?" asked Emmy.

Tom shook his head. "I don't believe it's safe to burn, dump, or blow it up. The only thing we can do is bury it, and I'm too tired to think of how or where."

"Why not right here?" asked Lee. She mostly was quiet during their meetings, seldom proposing ideas or solutions, but she was detailed and organized and ran a tight ship where their supplies were concerned.

Heads swiveled at her comment, which seemed to embarrass her a bit, but she went on. "Why not? Once this final project is complete, we'll either be moving on or dead, so afterwards, right before we all head out, we'll blow the prison - with, of course, VADER, still down in the lab."

Emmy nodded thoughtfully. "It could work. Sam? How are we sitting on explosives?"

"We're okay. We'd just have to take out the Annex."

"All right then," said Emmy. "That's settled. Tom, you'll have to break down the lab, of course, and pack up. Bart and Dave can help with that, and we'll set you up at Roseland. Just four weeks to go, folks. Let's hope it will be a very merry Christmas this year."

***

When Jules came to, she was still in the chair, with three large men clustered around her, desperately fanning her face and lightly slapping her palms. She shook them off and started to speak, then blinked several times before gathering her thoughts.

"How long was I out?" she asked.

"Couple minutes," George said, worry etched on his face.

"I'm fine," Jules said. "It was just a shock, that's all." They didn't look convinced, but she ignored that for now. She didn't see Frank slip out the door.

"All right. So I'm a target. We've always known they were going to try to retaliate at some point, although I never thought they'd actually pull it off. And Father Timothy . . ." Her voice trailed off. She mentally shook herself.

"We need to get a squad together, now, and go tonight. I'll go back to the house and tell them what's going on, and load up. We'll leave at sunset." She stood up and walked to the door, only to be stopped by Rosa's entrance.

"No, no, no, bambina! You come back to the house with me, and that is where you stay!"

Jules glared at her, but it did not good.

"You come with me, now."

"Fine," snapped Jules, but without any real venom. She was very tired from her brief fainting spell, too tired to argue. "Just give me five minutes!"

Rosa backed off about two steps and stood there, waiting, arms crossed over her chest and very nearly tapping her foot in impatience. Jules almost laughed at the caricature she presented. But then she put business first, as always.

"Go up there and take care of them. Tonight. Report to me the minute you get back."

Then she was ready to go.

Jules obediently followed Rosa back to the house and even allowed herself to be tucked into bed like an invalid. For now. EJ and Elizabeth came to keep her company, and even Storm stopped in for a few minutes. She spoke quietly with Jules, who immediately became very sleepy, and later, when she awoke, she could have sworn that the woman had cast some voodoo on her. On the other hand, she'd gotten some of the best sleep in her life, so voodoo or not, she wasn't going to dwell on it. Besides, Storm wasn't Cajun; she was Native American. From out West.

And that thought reminded her of David. It had been a good six months since he'd left, and Jules wondered where he was, or if he was even alive. She supposed she might see him again someday, but more than likely he was just another casualty of Co-OpCom.

She didn't think about them much either anymore. They'd been left alone for a year now, here in St. Louis, and the only chopper in sight was the one they'd captured. She worried, though, that everyone was becoming too complacent, even though they all thought that the government was pulling in, holing up in Chicago. But what would happen if this move strengthened them, helped them to increase their numbers and move out again? St. Louis was pretty darn close. With all the rebuilding, it might make a tempting target.

There was a knock at her door, and Bruno entered. He looked haggard, having stayed up all night to guard the door to Jules' room while he supervised patrols up and down the street. "George is back," he said.

"Five minutes," Jules told him, reaching for her clothes. "I'll be right there."

Bruno escorted Jules into the office, but she already knew things had gone wrong; she'd seen the men standing around, their downcast eyes and lowered heads. George's first words told her how very wrong it had been.

"Jules, we lost three men last night - Bill, Peter, and Marco. The gang was waiting and got the jump on us. I should've known they'd expect us right after what they did here, and I could have been ready for this."

"You couldn't have done anything, George," said Bruno fatalistically. "It was just one of those things."

"You weren't there!" shouted George. He was angrier and more out of control than Jules had ever seen him. "I let the men down, I let Mario down, and that is unacceptable." He took a deep breath and turned to Jules.

"With your permission, of course, I have a plan. A better plan. But first, I think you should leave the city. I've discussed it with Bruno and Frank, and they agree. A turf war is no place for a woman."

"Excuse me?" said Jules. She meant it, too. Surely she'd heard wrong.

"No, Jules," George told her. "That's exactly what I said. You have to leave."

And two days later, she did.

Chapter Twenty-Five

The way George had explained it to her made sense, but Jules was still fuming. She wasn't concerned in the least with leaving things in his hands, but she wanted to stay and fight. These were the people who had killed Mario, left her child fatherless. She was angry, yes, but she wanted revenge. Personally.

And it was all about this baby. She understood that they all wanted to protect her, and the baby, but still . . . she saw no reason why she had to leave. Bruno and Frank could stop anyone, and if she stayed, she could fight too.

But no. Rosa threw a fit when she found out that the gang had sworn to kill Jules, and she moved faster than Jules had ever seen her move in order to get everything and everyone ready to leave. EJ, Elizabeth, Storm, and Rosa were loaded into the chopper with all their supplies and were only waiting on Jules. She had a few things to go over with George, and then she'd be ready too.

"George, promise me that as soon as you get this taken care of, you'll come get me. I'm going to go stir-crazy down there with nothing to do and not knowing what's happening here. Promise!"

George sighed. "Jules, yes, I promise. But this might take some time. Stay safe, stay out of trouble, and take care of yourself. As soon as it's safe, Bruno will come after you." He kissed her on both cheeks and walked her to the waiting chopper.

Bruno was their pilot. Ever since the Miami trip, he'd been practicing, and he couldn't wait to show Jules. She'd never seen him exhibit so much excitement and interest over anything the last few months. She took the copilot seat, and the chopper rose over the city, banked, and flew south.

Looking out the window, Jules could see the entire area spread out before her. The remains of the Arch. The devastation throughout the county. One tiny pocket near the river where first Mario, and then she, had begun to rebuild. Then it was gone.

They landed thirty minutes later in the meadow, near the ruins of the old infirmary.

EJ was happy to be back. She'd been born here, grew up here, and wasn't very fond of big cities. Rosa, on the other hand, looked around fearfully. She'd never been outside the city, and nature was a foreign concept to her. She stayed close to the others, sometimes uncomfortably close, and jumped at every tweet or whistle or rustling in the long grass.

Jules found the camp to be much the same. It hadn't been that long since she and Abby and EJ had fled to Labadie when Colonel Hoefer came looking for them. And they'd been back since; they'd lived here for a short time before Walt was killed and the kids were taken. She glanced at Elizabeth, checking to make sure the girl wasn't having any kind of setback. Her group had been leaving, just over the hill to the south, when Co-OpCom descended upon them.

Storm was in her element. She stepped out of the chopper and raised her face to the sun, spread her arms wide, and muttered prayers. Or incantations. Or spells. Jules wasn't sure which, and she didn't really care. She was busy overseeing the unloading while EJ led Rosa and Bruno to the cave.

"Ayeee!" cried Rosa when she saw her new accommodations. She had lived in a nice house before VADER had destroyed her neighborhood and Colonel Barton had blown up the tree-lined street. She had lived in a warehouse, a brewery, and then the DeMenil Mansion, which even she admitted was more than what she'd been used to before. But this? A cave? In the middle of the country? It was almost too much to stand.

She stood there, arms akimbo, shaking her head. This - this place was going to take a lot of work to make it livable. She clapped a hand to the back of her neck and screeched when she saw the size of the spider smashed into her palm.

"It's okay," EJ told her. "It's just a wolf spider. It's harmless."

"It is now," snapped Rosa. "Oh, how will we ever live down here?"

"I was born here, you know," EJ said. "I lived here my whole life until I was six."

"Surely, child, you're making up stories. No one has ever been born in a cave, not since way back, a long time ago."

"Well, that's kind of true, I guess," EJ relented. She pointed down the hill to a stand of cedar trees. "I wasn't actually born in the cave, but by those trees over there. You can ask Jules. She was there. She helped my mom."

Rosa threw up her hands in defeat as Jules came into the clearing. "Ask Jules what?" she said as she lowered two packs to the ground.

"I was telling Rosa how I was born here and we lived here for years and years. I don't think she believes me," sighed EJ.

"Oh, it's true," Jules said. "After Abby took me and ran, we came up here. And then, er, Noah came back and EJ was born. It'll be fine, Rosa. Really, it will. Come on, let me show you the inside."

They finished the tour just as the others reached the cave. Rosa felt a little better after seeing the spacious main area of the cave and the adjoining chambers for sleeping and storage. A little better, but not much.

Elizabeth had never been to the cave, but seemed calm and composed as she arranged bedding and supplies. Jules was relieved and told herself she'd have a talk with the teenager as soon as they all got settled in, just to be on the safe side. Bruno was staying overnight to ensure that they had everything they needed and to help set up and gather a supply of firewood to get them started.

Storm had asked if she could set up her own camp, outside. Jules was concerned about the cold nights, but the woman just smiled and said, "The older I am, the more I become in touch with my people of long ago. I will be fine." Jules shrugged. It was a free country and all that. Well, sort of. At any rate, there was no reason for Storm not to do this.

Jules was curious about the woman, and since Rosa and Bruno kept shooing her away from doing any real work, she walked over to the stand of cedars that Storm had chosen for her campsite.

"This is where EJ was born," she said.

Storm nodded. "Good medicine here. The Spirit will be pleased."

"Spirit?" asked Jules, unsure what she was getting into by asking.

"The Great Spirit," Storm told her. "He who created all and watches over all."

"I see," said Jules. "Like God."

"No, He is God. Not like God. Same being, different name."

The two of them worked in companionable silence as they strung up a hammock and hung various bags of herbs and medicines above it. Storm found some rocks and made a small fire circle, and they filled it with twigs and a few larger sticks.

"Tell me your story, Storm. Where did you live, before VADER?"

"Come, sit," said the older woman. They sat by the fire circle, and Storm produced two pieces of flint, which she struck together repeatedly. When the tinder caught, she delicately blew on the sparks until there were flames, and then tossed a handful of crushed herbs onto the fire. A thin tendril of smoke rose into the air. And then she told Jules her story.

"Once, I was a teacher. In Chicago, in the city. Long before VADER, there were problems. When I was a young child, students respected teachers. Children were taught using the same methods. Some were brighter than others, and it was accepted that not all would be equally successful or choose the same path.

"Then someone decided that every student should be the same, that all had equal intelligence, and that everything must be changed to make things fair. No matter how many of us tried to explain that some students would never be rocket scientists, the powers that be insisted we were wrong. We struggled along, many of us losing our jobs because not all of our students showed brilliance. And then it got worse.

"Co-OpCom began to hand down certain curricula that we were forced to teach. Not only was it a requirement, but actual officers of the government were present in our classrooms all day long to make sure we complied. And it wasn't just the subject matter, but indoctrination of the Co-OpCom platform.

"I tried to resign, but none of us were allowed to do so. Finally, one day, I simply disappeared."

Jules thought about this for a few minutes. It certainly made sense. Abby hadn't been a teacher, but a coach, and in a far different area than Chicago. When Jules was growing up, Abby never lamented the lack of formal schooling, and now Jules had an idea why.

"But," she asked, "what about your family? Your friends?"

"Long ago, my grandparents left the reservation to make a better life for themselves and their children. My parents struggled in the white communities, but persevered until my siblings and I were adults. I've always known of my heritage and tried to live it as much as possible. But, like many young people, I was ready for a change, and so I moved into the city. After I left, I lost touch with everyone I'd ever known. And then I stumbled upon Riley, or, as you know her, Emmy."

Jules still hadn't decided how that all happened, the Riley-Emmy thing, but she supposed that sooner or later she'd hear more. And yes, she'd see Emmy soon too, after all this time. It wouldn't be long now before the plans in Chicago were underway. And would be successful, she hoped.

Chapter Twenty-Six

The countdown was on. Just one week left until the president arrived in Chicago.

Supplies had been cached near Plano and Morris for the groups traveling out of the area afterward, and more had been stashed near Roseland for those who were staying. Jerome had returned to the city to gather the tunnel people and present the plans to them.

Emmy called them all into one last meeting to go over all the details. After this, they were on their own until they'd come together in Millennium Park, in the heart of Chicago.

It was a somber group. They'd lived and worked and fought together for many years, and now it was coming to an end, one way or another. Emmy was relieved that it was nearly over. Abby, too. Alison was keyed up and bouncing around, the most animated of them all. She couldn't wait to get ahold of that bitch, Kat. Seriously couldn't wait.

Brad had mixed emotions. Sure, he wanted Co-OpCom destroyed, and he, too, was anxious to return to some semblance of normalcy. But he wondered about his relationship with Alison, now that all the excitement was coming to an end.

One way or another.

He wasn't afraid to die. But he was afraid of leaving her, and Jules, and all the rest of them. In many ways he was glad he'd never had children of his own, although Jules was like a daughter to him by every definition except biological. But the thought of leaving them, all of them, was weighing on him. He pulled Alison aside after everyone else had left.

"What's the plan?" he asked.

"Plan?" said Alison. "You know the plan: Go into the city, take them all down."

"No, not that. Us. You and me."

Alison looked startled. "What about us? Aren't we going back to St. Louis? To Jules? What's wrong?"

"Not that either. I mean us, what's going to happen to us when all the excitement dies down?" Brad looked troubled, but Alison was darned if she could make the connection.

"Look," said Brad. "You hated my guts when we first met, and then, well, things happened. And ever since, we've either been on the run or looking for trouble. So what happens when we settle down into a real life?"

"Oh. That."

"Yes, that. What do you think, Ali? Can we make this work?"

"Well, of course, silly! What, did you think I was in this just for an excuse to run around and shoot people and have someone to carry all the extra ammo?" She stood on her tiptoes and kissed him, then walked away, calling behind her, "I'll catch up with you in a bit!"

Brad wasn't satisfied with her response, but it would have to do. For now.

They all left for Roseland after sunset one evening. Gene and Brad stayed behind to conceal the chopper after they set down, and the others proceeded on foot several blocks. The safe house was still standing, but barely, after the south-side bombings.

Lee took them all downstairs and handed out uniforms - Co-OpCom uniforms. Tomorrow, they would don these and go into the city. Larry's people would be gathered just outside the park, near the Lurie Garden, waiting for the choppers to arrive.

One would carry the   president. One would carry his trusted advisor, General Kathleen Scott.

And one would carry the rebels, the resistance. They would have one shot at this, so to speak.

Abby and Emmy sat outside on the back steps, silently gazing up into the night sky. It was clear and cold, a perfect December evening.

"Do you think we'll ever see this again?" Emmy asked wistfully.

Abby put her arm around her old friend. "Yes. But hopefully from back home, and not anywhere near Chicago."

Emmy put her head on Abby's shoulder and leaned against her. They sat there for a very long time.

***

The chopper rose into the air, rotors furiously whipping the grass in the meadow. The women below waved goodbye to Bruno as he flew back to St. Louis.

"Now what?" wondered Rosa.

"Work first, then play," said Jules. She knew she was safe out here; it wasn't like Co-Op was coming, and those gangbangers wouldn't set foot out of the city. Heck, this was almost like a vacation. Besides, the busier she was, the less she'd think about what was happening in St. Louis. Or Chicago.

With that in mind, she assigned EJ and Elizabeth to gather more firewood. She ignored Rosa's protests about doing hard labor "in your condition," and left Storm to deal with the well-meaning woman. Jules was going exploring, as she hadn't been able to do in forever, it seemed.

She took some food and water, but assured them all that she'd be back before dark. She walked a bit slower these days and had to stop a few more times. This baby was really getting in the way. And besides that, her jeans were awfully uncomfortable, even when she left the snap undone.

Jules first went all the way back past the old campsites where they'd lived when she was a child, back into the woods to the spring. She looked around at the brown, dead branches and wished it was spring already. She knelt down awkwardly to get a drink and fill a bottle, and then she walked back into the woods further still, until she reached the cave. They'd blown the entrance right before they left the last time, but she knew there was still a cache buried inside. It hadn't been disturbed, and the fresh two-year growth almost made it unrecognizable.

She slung her pack over her shoulder and turned to walk back out into the late-morning sun, down the gravel path, nearly completely filled with weeds. She paused at the bridge over the creek, but didn't cross it. That's where she'd first stayed, with Grammy, before they lost some folks and the storage area had been blown up; before they all moved into one campsite, for safety.

Next, she came to the place she had called home for several years. Two? Four? She couldn't quite remember, but it didn't matter. She climbed the hill to Abby's tent, where she'd first learned about guns and shooting. She smiled at the memory of Abby telling her to never, ever touch even the case without an adult right there with her.

She sat down on the steps, ignoring the rotting canvas, and watched a line of ants march by as she remembered the past. Noah. Ted. Cal. Sandy. David. At last, she stood up, adjusted her gear and her gun, and climbed the hill, going higher and higher. When she reached the top, she stood very still for several minutes, taking it all in.

This is where Zoe had died that terrible winter. And her baby. Jules shivered. She remembered Brad's grief. She remembered how Noah had tried to save them. She didn't understand much, but she knew. And now, was it her turn? What would happen to her, and to her baby?

And then she felt something.

Wait, there it was again. She put her hand on her stomach, lightly, almost fearfully. Oh, yes, this was real. Her baby was definitely real. Tears came to her eyes as she thought of Mario. No one else, and nothing else.

She left the old campsite and went back - back to the cave, back to the living and those who were present.

Robin Tidwell

Chapter Twenty-Seven

The mountain air was sharp and thin and whipped through his many layers of clothing as he struggled against it. With a sharp bang, he shoved the door closed and dropped an armful of wood near the old stove. He pulled off his gloves and rubbed his hands together vigorously to try to bring back circulation. After a few minutes, he was able to flex them without too much pain.

He was alone and lonely, although he had everything he needed. After months spent finding this old cabin, filling in the cracks, repairing the sagging roof, he'd been able to hunt and gather and store enough food to last through the winter. Thanks to the previous owners, he had plenty of clothing and blankets. And firewood, although, in retrospect, he should have put the woodpile closer to the door.

Next year, he'd know better.

He'd traveled thousands of miles, mostly walking, although he once came across a rusty bicycle and thought, what the hell, how hard can it be? Turns out that it could be very hard indeed. The front tire blew within half a mile and he'd tumbled down a rocky embankment. So yes, mostly walking, except for half a mile or so.

He'd seen the ocean, the desert, the valleys, the mountains. A lot of mountains. And lakes, streams, rivers, and creeks. He'd seen tumble-down farmhouses and abandoned fields, heavy equipment left in those fields to stand as rusted, hulking monuments to their late owners.

He'd crossed railroad tracks, over and over. It seemed like the same ones, but the weeds were different and grew in diverse patterns, and he knew they couldn't be the same ones. Surely not.

He'd shared a cave with a lone wolf for two weeks, and then one day the wolf didn't come back.

He saw vacant motels, and highways littered with cars and trucks and motorcycles and eighteen-wheelers. He saw big cities full of broken glass and broken signs and broken bridges. He saw more derelict buildings than he, or anyone, could ever accurately count.

He'd been to Phoenix, to San Diego, to Vegas, and to Denver. He'd even walked through Area 51. No aliens. And no people. None at all. Zip. Nowhere.

And he'd been to LA. More accurately, he'd climbed the hill to the remains of the Hollywood sign. The entire metro area was dark. He'd hunkered down in the brush and waited until morning. And there, he saw people.

Before VADER, the Los Angeles area was home to nearly eighteen million people. Based on what he knew, afterward there should have been maybe one million. There weren't that many now. He suspected gang activity, general ineptitude in a situation such as no one before had ever faced, and the usual death and disease combined with a low, or even nonexistent, birthrate. Maybe he didn't have a lot of formal education, but he did read a lot. Always had.

He got the hell out of Los Angeles as quick as he could and went back to the mountains. This is where he would stay, alone. He spent his days fixing up the cabin, exploring the area, and getting ready for winter. Sometimes he wished he had a dog, but few had been seen since VADER, and most of those had gone wild since their owners died or disappeared.

In the evenings, he mostly stared at the fire until it died down, thinking. Remembering. He'd once lived with people - special people, people who loved him. But he'd wanted adventure, and so he left. And he had adventure, all right. And most of the time, he preferred it this way.

Lately, though, he'd been wondering. Wondering if it was possible to go back in time, and in space. Wondering if she was still there, still alive. Alone, like him.

He'd think about it. He had all winter, as the passes, particularly Wolf Creek, were closed up tight, snow-packed and icy. Maybe come March, if the weather broke for a few days. Maybe.

In the meantime, he had come across another cabin just before the blizzards came. This one was in better shape than his own and he wished he'd found it first, but he was pretty well settled in now and didn't want to move. He'd found a box of notebooks, empty ones, spiral, the kind he used in school when he was a kid. Before VADER.

Maybe he'd write it all down. VADER. His story, and hers. Maybe he'd give it a happy ending.

Maybe.

Robin Tidwell

Chapter Twenty-Eight

Gene flew the chopper in low and set it down smoothly. The crowds milling around the park were subdued and oddly quiet. When they stepped out, a mass wave of retreat rippled through those present as they took a collective step backward.

Fear, Abby thought. If they only knew.

She and the others moved to the stage, ringing its base, standing at attention. Those in the front of the crowd blended together, except for Larry's people. They were there. They were ready, front and center.

Choppers. Two of them.

They landed. The engines were cut. The rotors stopped.

Bodyguards exited first, weapons at the ready. They surrounded their subjects, moving toward the stage. Once there, they formed a line between the stage and the crowd. They ignored what they presumed to be their fellow mercenaries. Their leader approached Emmy and saluted.

"We appreciate your attention to detail. We had not expected such a strong additional presence of our soldiers. Carry on."

He joined the ranks along the edge of the crowd.

They were all somewhat baffled. If they'd known it would be this easy to impersonate the troops . . .

They snapped to attention. The president and his advisor were ascending the steps. They reached the stage itself and turned to wave.

Why bother, thought Alison bitterly. Not like anyone was going to wave back. Surprisingly, some few did. There were no shouts, but no demonstrations of discontent.

Suddenly, a shot rang out. The tunnel people. Right on schedule.

The crowd panicked and began milling about, pushing against the front line of soldiers, who were quick to swing their guns and shove back. Some fired, which increased the terror. Another shot, far back in the crowd. More panic, more shoving, more commotion for the mercenaries to deal with.

The rebels weren't idle. At the first shot, they surrounded the president and his advisor and, on Emmy's signal, moved as one unit toward the choppers. The engines fired, and the rotors began to turn. Brad flung open the door, and Bart and Jim boosted their hostages inside. The others followed, and the chopper rose into the air.

And it hovered, some 30 feet off the ground.

"What?" exclaimed the president. "What are you doing? Why aren't we going anywhere? I demand that you fly out of this area immediately!"

"All in good time, Mr. President," said Emmy. She nodded toward Bart, who pulled out his Sig and centered the barrel on the president's forehead. Emmy almost smiled at his expression. Jim swiftly bound the captive's hands and feet.

"What are you doing to him?" shrieked General Scott. She lunged for Bart, but Brad grabbed her arm, throwing her balance off and sending her sprawling.

Alison lifted her face shield and peered at the woman on the floor. "Hello, Kat," she said sweetly, and followed that with a roundhouse punch that knocked the advisor out cold.

Emmy turned her attention back to the president.

"I don't know if you remember me, and I don't really care. I could tell you the whole story, but I don't need to. I lived it. You caused it.

"Your regime is finished. In just a minute, we're going to set down in the middle of that crowd. And we're going to end it all."

"What? What are you planning? You can't do this! I'm the president!"

Emmy took out a syringe.

"What is that? That's not - "

"Yes, it is, Mr. President. What's good enough for the people is good enough for you. Or something like that. I don't really care. I'm tired."

And indeed Emmy looked exhausted. Abby moved closer, just in case. She tapped Emmy on the shoulder and looked at her questioningly.

"I can do this," Emmy told her. "I'm all right. It's personal, after all."

Gene called back from the cockpit, "Are you about done back there? We're ready to set down." He'd flown directly above the crowd, who had been moved back in a circle by the soldiers on the ground.

Bart and Jim hauled the president to his feet as the chopper touched down. When the rotors stopped turning, they dragged him to the open doorway. Emmy stood next to him, syringe in hand.

"This," she shouted, "is your president. He is not mine. The things he has done to me, I can't begin to relate to you in just a few minutes. And minutes are all we have. All he has."

"This," she held up the syringe, "is his new pet project. His new VADER."

A rumble swept through the crowd. They moved back.

"Oh, it will only hurt you if you're injected," Emmy told them. "Those vans over there, that's where you were going to go after this rally. They hold trunks full of these syringes, except it isn't actually VADER. We took care of that. VADER is in a safe place, never to be found. Ever."

Another rumble from the crowd, this one louder. And longer.

When it stopped, Emmy grabbed the president's arm. She raised the syringe. She stabbed his arm.

And pressed the plunger.

The president remained still as Bart and Jim released him and stepped back into the shadows. Emmy dropped the syringe and leaned against the door, watching the man who had caused such suffering and grief and death. So much death.

He opened his mouth to speak, but the roar of the crowd drowned out any words he might have spoken. He took a staggering step and fell to the ground. As he tried to rise, the crowd moved in, closer and closer. The soldiers could no longer hold them back, and most had stopped trying.

The president rose to his feet and clawed at his chest. He pulled out a small derringer and swung it around toward Emmy. He fired. She slumped to the floor.

And then it began. The first drop of blood appeared on his face.

Cracks ripped across his skin as he screamed. He fell to his knees. He writhed in agony. He begged and pleaded. The

RECYCLED

screams stopped. And then he was gone. Completely gone. All that remained was a pile of bloody rags.

Abby had rushed to Emmy's side and dragged her away from the door. "Let's go!" she shouted to Gene. The chopper started and lifted as Abby bent to examine Emmy's wound.

She let out a sigh of relief. It was merely a flesh wound, high on her chest, just a grazing, really. Among other things, the president hadn't been noted for his marksmanship. She rubbed Emmy's hands, trying to bring her back to consciousness. Within a minute, Emmy sat up.

"What happened?"

Abby hugged her tightly. "You did it, Em. And we're done. We're leaving."

"Not exactly done," piped up Alison, nudging Kat's still form with her boot.

"Is she still out?" asked Abby.

"Yeah," said Alison. "I might have had to smack her again. Might have." She grinned.

"Well, wake her up!" snapped Abby.

"Sure thing," said Alison, tossing the contents of a water bottle into Kat's face. The woman woke up sputtering and swinging. "Easy there," Alison told her, pushing her back down with a booted foot. "Brad's got you covered, you piece of crap. One more move and he'll blow out your brains."

"No, he won't," said Kat smugly. "You want to do that yourself - probably after you torture me and get me to tell you things. Well, I won't do it!"

Alison laughed. "Really? What are you going to not tell me that we don't already know? The new supply of VADER? Plans to kill off most of your ardent supporters? Oh, wait, they aren't very ardent anymore, are they?"

Kat's face paled.

"By the way, your president is dead. Emmy here, she stuck him with one of those syringes that are so popular these days. Yep, right in front of those 'ardent supporters.' They all know now, Kat. Last we saw, lifting off, they were swarming all over those soldiers of yours. Too bad.

"Gene," she called. "Are we ready?"

"Yes, ma'am. Twelve hundred feet up."

"Ready for what?" asked Kat fearfully. Then she tossed her head and glared at them all. "Doesn't matter. I know you want to shoot me, Alison. You were always jealous of my rise in rank, my promotions. You just hung out with the wrong crowd, those losers like Eric and Marta."

Alison fired.

Kat looked around in disbelief, then down at her shoulder. "Lousy aim, too," she said sarcastically.

"Oh, no," said Alison. "I have excellent aim. That was for Eric." She fired again, shattering Kat's thigh. "And that was for Marta."

She took two steps toward Kat and looked down at her pitilessly. "This is for me." She yanked Kat to her feet and shoved her out the open door, Brad grabbing onto her before the force of it sucked her out too.

And she watched Kat fall.

The chopper banked and went south to Roseland.

Chapter Twenty-Nine

They waited at the safe house for five days before Jerome arrived.

"Sorry it took me so long," he said, "Larry wanted me to wait until we had all the info.

"So, after you all took off, everyone just stood there. Real quiet-like. And then, when that general fell out of the chopper, man, you should have heard the screams! Good aim, too. She landed about twenty feet away from the president.

"Anyway, a few people started poking around the bodies, or what was left, and one of the soldiers, I guess he was in charge, he made them all step back. He looked them over and shook his head. Then he called all the troops and they had, like, this big huddle or something.

"Then he grabbed a big bullhorn and told all the people to just go on home. Some of them did, I guess, but most just gathered up in groups, talking about what happened. Our people kind of walked around, listening in."

"What about the troops?" asked Gene.

"Huh. Funny thing. I heard them talking about their pay and wondering who was in charge now. Finally, one them said, Hey, let's go over to the Daley Center and find out. So they did. Pete, he followed them at a distance and said they went on inside. So he snuck in and wandered around a little until he heard voices.

"While he was waiting out in the hall, he heard a bunch of firing, so he ducked into a closet. When it sounded like everyone had left and it got all quiet again, he came out. The soldiers were all gone, but the room was full of bodies. Lot of blood, too."

Abby and Emmy exchanged looks. Sounded like the entire cabinet had been assassinated.

"Anyone left alive?" Emmy asked.

"Nope, not that Pete could tell, but he didn't stick around long. He heard choppers taking off, and he ran down the stairs and out the door, just in time to see them lift off."

"Which direction did they go?"

"Pete said west. And there were two more choppers. Four altogether."

"Well," said Alison, "they aren't sticking around here, for sure. Guess that whole mercenary dynamic kind of fell apart. I say we don't worry about it. They're gone, the government is dead, time to move on."

Emmy nodded slowly. "I'm sure you're right. Jerome? What about the people?"

"Well," he said, scratching his head, "it was weird. Some of them just took off out of the area, but not very many. Most of them stood around, talking, in small groups. They all kind of seemed at a loss, but no one was upset or crying or anything.

"After a while, Larry picked up one of those bullhorns - a soldier must've dropped it - and he climbed up on some steps over by the Lurie Garden. He started talking, and after a few minutes a lot of them came over to see what he had to say."

"Any opposition?" asked Lee. "And what about numbers? How many are staying in the area?"

"Let's see," said Jerome, unfolding a piece of paper. "Larry gave me this so I wouldn't forget. He said about 200 or so are staying, and the rest are making plans to go back to wherever they came from. He asked everyone there to kind of let him know and told them all that they were welcome to stay, or come back later. And he gave this big speech about freedom and how we have it now and how no one's in charge, but we gotta all work together."

"Sounds like Larry's found his calling," said Abby, smiling.

"Oh, there were a lot of questions, but he answered a bunch of them. And then pretty much everyone left. So I stuck around for a week, and then Larry sent me down here. Oh, and I'm supposed to give you this." He handed Emmy another piece of paper.

She opened it, skimmed it, and handed it to Tom.

"'We the people,'" he read, and looked up. "No, it's not the Constitution, but Larry's own manifesto. Has a good ring to it!

"All right, I'm ready to go. Lee?"

She nodded. "Yes, time to start over. Jerome, are you ready to go back home?"

"You betcha! I'm just glad we can come out of the tunnels now and have a real place to live. Man, that got old fast. But . . . what about the rest of you? Are you gonna come back and visit sometime?" He looked at Abby. "I promise not to pull a gun or anything on you next time."

She gave Jerome a hug and told him she wasn't worried. If he did, she'd just shoot him right away. He took a step back before he realized she was joking. Probably.

Tom and Lee said their goodbyes too; Emmy last. Her shoulder was healed but still stiff. "Keep exercising that, Emmy," Tom told her. "And if you all need me for anything, send Gene up here. I'll come right away."

She nodded, not trusting herself to speak. They'd been together a long time, and this wasn't easy. St. Louis to Chicago hadn't been a long distance to travel back when the highways were intact and the trains were running, but it may as well be thousands of miles now. The chopper was running on fumes already, and the spare fuel was long gone.

She watched until they were out of sight.

Bart and Jim were the next to leave, but they weren't starting out until morning. They were going west. Both felt the urge to wander and had been cooped up in basements and houses for far too long. They planned to take it easy, no hurry, do some hunting and fishing along the way. Maybe go to the coast. See what happened to Los Angeles. No rush, no real plans.

"Maybe you'll run into David," said Alison.

"Who's David?"

"A young man who lived with us in Missouri. We found him living nearby with an older man and Elizabeth and her brother. They had a nice setup in the woods, cabin and all, but then we had to leave . . ." Abby frowned, thinking.

"He went west," Brad told them. "Not sure where. Said he wanted to see what was going on out there. Of course, we haven't heard a thing, no way to send a message, but he was pretty resourceful."

"Well," said Bart, smiling, "it's a big country."

Two days later, the chopper lifted off from Roseland with Gene at the controls. Abby, Brad, Alison, and Emmy were going home.

They landed in St. Louis and looked around in surprise. No one was there.

Chapter Thirty

"Now what?" asked Alison. She was annoyed, expecting to see Jules, but more than that—what the heck had happened? Where was everyone? Damn creepy.

Emmy was staring out the front of the chopper, taking in the ruins of the city and shaking her head. As they'd crossed the river, she'd seen the leaning, rusty legs of the Arch, all that was left.

"We can't lift off," Gene said. "Out of fuel. We're sittin' ducks here." He looked around warily.

Suddenly, shots rang out. They all ducked down and reached for their weapons.

"Crap," said Abby.

More shots. People running. Shouts, and then screams.

No one dared raise his head to see what was happening, but in minutes the noise had stopped. A loud banging sounded on the door, and they heard George's voice.

"Gene! Are you guys in there? Everyone okay?"

Gene flung open the door. "What the hell is going on here?"

Alison shoved past him, Abby on her heels. "Where's Jules?"

"Hang on," George said. "The girls are fine, Jules and EJ both. Bruno just got back from a trip down there. We sent them away because of all this ruckus that you just landed in the middle of. Jules isn't in any condition to fight, and we knew if she were here, she'd jump right into it."

"What do you mean? Is she hurt?" Alison's eyes were wide as her voice rose an octave higher. Brad grabbed her arm and held tight.

"No, no, she's fine, but with the baby and all, she sure doesn't need to be getting shot at."

"Baby?" Alison shrieked. "Baby?" She turned to Gene. "You knew about this!"

Gene ducked behind George. "Now, Alison, calm down. She made me promise not to tell you; guess she wanted to be the first. I don't know, I just did, and I'm sorry. Really sorry," he added, when he saw her face, hoping she wouldn't shoot him just for fun.

Abby grabbed Alison's other arm. "Relax," she said, "I'm sure everything's fine."

"I would think so!" snapped Alison, wrenching away from both Brad and Abby. "But I'm certainly not old enough to be a grandmother!" She took off walking toward the brewery. By God, someone better have some alcohol around here.

Abby shrugged, tried to hide her smile, failed utterly. Brad had a goofy look in his face, but he snapped out of it when Alison called, "Are you coming, damn it?"

Emmy stepped out of the chopper, still trying to take it all in, and looked around as George's men dragged bodies out of the street. She greeted George and asked him about the gang war as they walked over to the office.

Alison found a drink, but it sure wasn't tequila; some home-brewed stuff that Big Frank made in a still out back. Had quite a kick, too, as they all discovered a few minutes later. She fell asleep in her chair while George brought them up to speed.

He told them about Mario and how Jules and Bruno had gone up north to retaliate. They thought the problem had been taken care of, but some months later, the gang became active again. They had a new leader and he wanted revenge. Specifically, he wanted Jules dead.

He and Bruno and Frank had discussed it at length and decided that Jules should leave. So they sent her and EJ, along with Rosa and Storm, down to the old camp. They'd been there about a month, and Bruno had gone down there twice already to check on them. Everything was fine.

"So," said Abby, "tell us more about this gang war."

"They hit us, they run." George shrugged. "Every time, though, we take out more of their men, and we've only had a few minor injuries ourselves. You happened to land at just the right moment for us. Those guys took off when they saw the chopper, but their curiosity got the better of them.

"They keep us busy down here. Usually they show up three or four times a week. Trying to wear us down, I guess, but we've got a lot of ammo. The problem is that we're spread kind of thin and we can't spare anyone to make a counteract. That's what we need to do, go after their leader, 'cause he won't show his face during the fighting. Sits up there in his own territory with a few bodyguards."

"How do you know all this? Do you have a name? A description?" Emmy looked intently at George, waiting for answers. Abby realized that this wasn't going to be a short visit. She sighed.

"Right before all this started, a kid showed up here. Well, we call him Kid now, and he works with Bruno. And no," he said, shaking his head, "Kid isn't leaking info to them. He spilled his guts when we first grabbed him, stealing food, and he sticks to Bruno like glue. In fact, he told us quite a lot about the gang right after that. But like I said, we've got all we can do here to protect the women and kids, and we never know when they'll hit. There's no pattern. What we need to do is send someone up there while most of them are busy here." George finished his monologue and sat back, waiting.

"All right," said Abby, looking at Emmy. "We'll start tonight. We'll flush 'em out and finish this once and for all."

Gene went to find Bruno to see about fuel, and Brad half carried, half dragged Alison over to the DeMenil Mansion. Jeanine was there, and she put Alison to bed before setting about making dinner for everyone.

Abby and Emmy stayed behind while George went over the map of the north side with them, showing them possible locations to investigate.

"This," he said, "is where Jules first went. Mullanphy Street. That was their old space, and we all thought the leader was there. But it was just one part of the gang, and apparently the part that included his brother.

"Our best guess is to start from there."

"Got it."

They walked north up Interstate 55 because it was the most direct route into enemy territory. They had no real intel on whether or not the gang would strike that night, but George hazarded a guess that they might, just because of their casualties earlier that day. At any rate, the first step was to locate them.

The highway was ruined, of course, but passable on foot. Alison wasn't in any mood to climb, and she griped and grumbled for the first two miles, wondering aloud just what Frank put in that whiskey. Her head was killing her.

When they reached the confluence of 55 and 44, the massive pile of steel and concrete gave them pause. Seeing all the destruction up close like this was unreal. Emmy hadn't been here for so long that she was very nearly lost in the maze of destruction.

It was cold that night, but they barely felt it as they kept walking up Tucker to Market, stopping right at the doors of City Hall.

"Okay," said Abby. "We can keep going up Tucker to Mullanphy, but the buildings that fell likely blocked the streets, and it's going to be rough going. If we move west and cut through the residential areas, it might be quicker from here on out."

Brad rubbed his hands together to warm them. "Sounds good to me. Been standing here too long anyway, or it's getting colder. Let's move."

"Hang on," Abby told him. "We know the general area that they've been in, unless they've moved, and in which case we're out of luck, and we know where they used to be. So I think we should separate when we get, say, to Washington. Two of us can go up 18th, two of us up 14th."

They walked as far as Lucas Park, a block south of Washington, and then Brad and Alison went west a few blocks to 18th Street.

Abby and Emmy heard the gang long before they spotted the building from where the sound was emanating. The old Carr School. It had been run-down and derelict long before VADER. But it hadn't taken a direct hit during the Colonel Barton era, and was probably at least minimally functional.

Abby doubled back and looped around to 18th, catching up with Brad and Alison. The three of them retreated to the park and waited for Emmy. She'd insisted on being the one to move in closer. After the brisk jog over seven blocks, Abby was wishing she'd argued.

Emmy returned at a trot. "Sounds like they're drinking and partying it up. Maybe getting ready to go south, probably not. Maybe it's their version of a wake? Whatever. Two choices: Move back farther and wait, maybe go back for reinforcements, or move in after they all pass out."

"Aw, let's just get it over with," said Brad. "I'm tired of lowlife scum. We took down Co-OpCom; we can handle a few gangbangers."

They moved cautiously north, just to the southeastern edge of Loretta Hall Park. Bet no one ever thought these pocket areas of greenery would be used like this, thought Abby, although she remembered the homeless problem long ago, back before VADER—and probably immediately after—and thought twice.

Around three o'clock in the morning, the shouts abated and voices became quieter. Lights were extinguished, one by one. And then silence reigned.

The four of them spread out along the back of the building and pulled bricks of C4 from their packs. Working quickly, they stuffed the malleable explosive into cracks along the back wall, from Carr Street to 15th. They connected the detonators and cord and moved back to the far corner of the block, behind a pile of rubble that had come from who knew where.

BOOM!

Pieces of debris rained down around them, but they didn't stay still long enough to worry about being hit. They scattered, Abby and Emmy going one direction, Brad and Alison the other, and they watched through the smoke and dust for any survivors.

BAM! One went down. Then another. And last, a big man came staggering out, rubbing his eyes, limping. He fell to the ground. Instantly, four guns were pointed at his head.

"Are you the lowlife scum trying to kill my daughter?" asked Alison.

"What? Who the hell are you?"

"Answer the question," Brad demanded.

"Oh, yeah, that bitch down south. She killed my brother. Screw you!"

"Oh, I don't think so," said Alison. "I have standards. And taste."

She fired.

"And I'm having a bad day."

Robin Tidwell

Chapter Thirty-One

Bruno went down to pick up Jules and the others, and Alison elected to go with him. They returned within hours. Rosa was so happy to be back that she fell to her knees, kissed the ground, crossed herself, then practically ran to the house to see Jeanine. Elizabeth was quiet and composed, as always, but surprised Abby by chattering away and taking an almost mothering approach to EJ. Or, as EJ would later tell her mother, "She's pretty bossy, just like she used to be."

Storm greeted Emmy and the others with little fanfare, as was her way. And then Jules, with Bruno's assistance, stepped out of the chopper.

Emmy's heart skipped a beat as she took in the tall, young woman, only a child when she had last seen her. And now having a child herself. She wasn't sure what to say or what to do, but Jules knew—she nearly flew across the open space that separated them and threw her arms around Emmy.

"All these years," she cried. "I didn't believe it, couldn't believe it, until just now!" She wiped away a tear and apologized. "I'm a little emotional these days."

But Emmy didn't care. She was crying openly, just as the old Emmy would have done. She had thought of Jules often during those dark years, remembering the little girl she'd once taken care of and taught and loved. But this was certainly no little girl.

"George," said Jules, "we'll meet in my office in an hour. I want to know everything that's happened in my absence. Make sure everyone is there."

Rosa and Jeanine outdid themselves for the celebration dinner that evening. There was much talk and laughter, and plans for the future were discussed. Alison and Emmy kept watching Jules and shaking their heads, occasionally catching each other's expressions and smiling in amazement.

To Alison, this long-lost daughter of hers was a continuing enigma; she was lost, then found, and had grown from a toddler into a self-sufficient young woman. Now she was about to become a mother herself and had taken over the leadership of an entire group of people. And was doing a bang-up job of it, too.

Emmy had helped raise Jules from a small girl of four, but had missed her coming of age. And, while she certainly saw flashes of the young girl, she was astounded at the outcome. Then again, her own experiences had changed and hardened her, and so she suspected that, with or without her presence, Jules may have been exactly the same. But it was hard to not feel sadness and a sense of loss for all she missed; for all both of them had missed.

For her part, Jules was simply trying to hold herself together. The reality of her situation was beginning to weigh on her. So many questions. She was comfortable with Alison, and the transition from Abby to Alison hadn't been difficult at the time. But now . . . this baby was causing a lot of problems, she thought. And there was Emmy, who she thought was dead, but wasn't.

216

Given her life up until now, none of this should be surprising or even noteworthy. She barely remembered Texas, where she was born, and the hardships after her father had abducted her left little impression. The arrival of VADER had been terrifying for everyone, but especially a four-year-old left alone. Abby had saved her. Jules suspected she had three mothers now, and that wasn't going to change, but she needed some time to figure things out. And there was never enough time.

She had some thinking to do, especially regarding the family. Mario's family. This baby was theirs as much as it was hers, but did she really want to spend the rest of her life here, in the city? She knew that Abby was anxious to leave, as were the others, but what did she herself want?

***

The next few months were a whirlwind of activity. The family continued to improve their living situation and to rebuild. More people began to trickle into St. Louis, survivors from Chicago who were looking for a change of scene. Most settled in with the family, although a few started their own communities nearby. There were no territories, no gangs, no fights or wars, simply small communities, clustered together, much like the St. Louis area had been . . . before VADER.

Of course, there were problems: the occasional theft, some arguments, a fistfight or three. But for the most part, people remembered VADER, and Co-OpCom, and swore they wouldn't make the same mistakes.

With the new people came new skills, new ideas. More little shops were opened, more buildings salvaged. A boat builder arrived, and he and Pete started a fishing group. Hunters went out into the country, which, as it must have been long before any of them had been born, was now located merely a few miles from the brewery itself.

Bruno still watched over Jules, a job becoming easier as her due date approached, and George took over more of her responsibilities.

"Bruno," said Jules one day in April, "don't you think this must have been what the Old West was like, a town like this? Whoever would have thought that St. Louis would be like this again?"

The big man nodded in agreement. "We've come a long way, Jules. Wish Mario were here to see it."

"Yes. He would be so proud." And then she doubled over in pain.

"Jules?"

"Yes," she gasped. Oh, no. Not now!

"Jules? Are you okay?" Bruno grabbed her arm and turned her around. He saw her face and was scared to death.

"I'm fine," she told him. "But I think it's time." Her face was pale and she was sweating.

Without another word, Bruno scooped her up and almost ran back to the house, shouting at passersby to move out of the way. Jules almost laughed at the expression on his face, and then another pain ripped through her body. That was nothing to laugh about.

Holy crap, this hurt!

Bruno leapt up the steps and crashed through the front door. Rosa came out of the kitchen, wiping her hands on a towel. Her jaw dropped, and she pointed to the stairs. Bruno took them two at a time and went down the hall to Jules' room. He set her gently on the bed and then stepped back, gasping for air.

The others crowded into the room. Alison went to her daughter and took her hand. Jules was panting, trying to ignore another pain. Damn, this hurt. Whose bright idea was this, anyway? She really wished Mario was here right now. She wasn't entirely sure why. She was kind of angry with him at this particular moment.

Unaware that her thoughts were exactly those of countless women who had given birth before her, Jules let out an involuntary moan. Oh, good Lord, her mother had gone through this? Why? And then she remembered the birth of EJ. Oh, crap.

Rosa clapped her hands and shooed everyone out into the hall. Alison glared at her. She was not moving from Jules' side, and that was the end of it. Rosa shrugged as she and Storm took over. They examined Jules, and Storm gave her a sip of her special tea. Jules dozed throughout the afternoon, as comfortable as they could make her.

Abby and Emmy waited downstairs. EJ and Elizabeth had been sent down to the river to get Brad, and they all arrived within an hour. The day dragged on. Alison came downstairs after a while to take a break, at the urging of Rosa and Storm, and she sent Abby back up in her place. Emmy elected to remain in the old parlor, waiting with Brad.

She almost laughed at him. He was pacing back and forth, wringing his hands, clearly worried, but it was so classic. She marveled aloud at how young he looked for someone about to become a grandpa. That broke the tension. A little. He smiled. A little.

"I probably look really silly, huh?"

"Yes," Emmy told him, "yes, you do. But I understand. I'm sure it won't be long now.

EJ, who'd been in the room she shared with Elizabeth, came rushing down the stairs and into the kitchen. Seconds later, Alison ran past and blew kisses and hollered, "It's time!"

Brad started pacing again.

Jules was in a bad way. She was hot, she was cold, she was shaking, she was in agony. Absolute agony. If she could have, she would have said, "This blows. I'm outta here!" But she couldn't. And so she groaned and writhed and tried to listen to Rosa's voice. Her mother was on one side of her and Abby on the other. She'd tried to leave when Alison came back, but Jules wanted her to stay.

"Of course," Alison said with a smile. "Wouldn't have it any other way!" Then she turned her attention back to her daughter. "Honey, I know it hurts. God knows, having you wasn't the easiest thing I've ever done, but I promise you, it was the best thing I ever did. It'll be worth it. And you're almost done." She squeezed Jules' hand.

Abby remained silent. She was pleased that Jules wanted her here, but she was sensitive to Alison's prerogative as her mother. She knew. But she held on tight to Jules, thinking of this wonderful girl who was like a daughter to her, who had helped her so much at EJ's birth even though she was a child herself.

The baby was coming.

Rosa was ready. Jules pushed with all her might. One more show of herculean strength and her baby was born. Rosa wiped off the tiny infant and deftly wrapped her in a blanket, handing her to Jules.

"A little girl," Rosa said, smiling broadly. "So tiny, and so perfect."

Jules stared at the bundle she held with an expression of mixed relief and confusion and happiness. Now what? She hadn't a clue. But she seemed to be holding the baby the right way. At least, this was how she remembered holding EJ. And she hadn't yet dropped her. That was something.

Wait a minute. Why does it still hurt? Isn't this supposed to be over?

Alison frowned at Jules' grimace of pain and gently took the baby as Storm summoned Rosa back to the foot of the bed. All she wanted to do was examine this new granddaughter of hers, and what the heck was going on down there anyway? She handed the baby to Abby and turned back to Jules, smoothing her hair, gripping her hand.

Abby gazed down at the child's face. Her eyes were barely open, squinting against the light, and Abby shaded her face with her hand. Blue eyes stared up at her. A shock of dark hair sprung from her tiny head. And then Jules cried out again. Abby jerked her attention back to the bed.

A loud wail came from the foot of the bed. Another baby.

"Twins!" exclaimed Rosa. "Two perfect little girls!"

"Holy crap!" said Jules and Alison, at the same time.

Brad and Emmy jumped up as Abby and Alison came down the stairs an hour later, each carrying a baby. Brad blinked. Emmy laughed in delight.

"Here you go, Grandpa." Alison set the baby in his arms. "This is Rosie."

"And this," said Abby, following suit, "is Millie."

Robin Tidwell

Chapter Thirty-Two

Within a month, Jules was starting to feel like her old self. It certainly helped that her babies had plenty of aunts and uncles and grandmas to help take care of them. And Grandpa. Jules giggled. Brad as a grandpa was still just too funny, for some reason. At any rate, sometimes she had to take them into her room and shut the door just to have a little alone time with them.

They continued to fascinate her—not as babies, particularly, but as her own. Little beings who were part of her . . . and Mario. She couldn't imagine anything different now that they'd arrived. Who knew? She asked herself, smiling.

She tucked them into their crib, the one Frank had built, and went downstairs. She could hear voices in the parlor, but they went silent when she entered the room.

"What? What's going on?" she asked, looking at each of them.

Brad cleared his throat and looked at the others. "We're talking about leaving. Going back to Walt's old place."

Jules looked around the room. "All of you?" she asked, not knowing exactly what else to say. "Why?"

Abby looked at Emmy. "Too much city for us here," she said. "And some bad memories. Sometimes the good just doesn't make the bad go away." She put a hand on Emmy's shoulder.

Her friend looked up at her, grateful for the explanation she'd given Jules. The transition from her alternate persona had been difficult for Emmy. She wanted so badly to be herself, to go back to the way things used to be, but Riley was hard to shake. She'd been born out of necessity, a second chance; a chance to overcome the things that had been done to her, had made her a victim.

It had taken a huge toll on her, physically and mentally. And the reunion with Jules had only underscored the differences between her old life and the one she wished to renew. It was time to take matters into her own hands, and she couldn't do it in St. Louis, not here, not where it had all started.

Jules looked lost, and Alison felt terrible about her own decision. She and Brad had talked at length, weighing the pros and cons, and made the decision together. It was time. Jules had her own life here. She was with her family, Mario's family, and she was just getting back into the swing of things since the babies' birth. Moreover, she was doing a fabulous job, one which became more complicated daily as more immigrants came to St. Louis and the population expanded. Alison would never ask Jules to leave, but she herself was ready to move on to . . . whatever came.

"And EJ? Elizabeth?"

The two girls nodded. Of course, EJ was not quite ten and would go with Abby, regardless. Elizabeth had been seeing a young man from the next community over, and Jules was surprised at her decision. Since she had no parents or guardians, the rest of them had more or less taken responsibility for Elizabeth. And when Jules realized that the girl was, yes, just sixteen, she understood. It was a little too young for her to be serious about anyone, even if times had changed and even if Charles was a nice young man. Which he was.

"I see," said Jules. "When were you planning to leave?"

"In two weeks," Alison told her gently.

"I see," Jules repeated, and walked out of the room. She didn't know what else to say, or what to do, or even what to think. Two weeks. Everyone was leaving her.

She spent a restless night, even when the babies were sleeping, and she awoke to find her pillow wet from tears. She'd dreamt of Mario. He was smiling and waving.

After a morning spent in her room, she finally emerged and went in search of Abby.

"I need to talk to you," she said.

Abby looked up from her list and told EJ to go find Alison. She knew why Jules was here. She'd seen the look on her face yesterday when they broke the news.

"I want to go with you."

Abby smiled. "Jules, honey, we'd love to have you—always, you know that. But you have a life here - your babies, Mario's family. They all need you to be here, to do what you're doing."

"No." Jules shook her head. "George is perfectly capable. In fact, if I hadn't been here, he would have been the one to take Mario's place. I only did it for him, for Mario. And I've done what he wanted. All of this - " she waved her hands, "was for him, a continuation of his dream."

Abby nodded. "I understand, Jules, I really do. Why you did it, and why you think you're ready to leave it behind. If you're sure, if you've made up your mind, none of us are against it. We were all hoping that you'd come with us, but it had to be your decision." She hugged the girl and kissed her cheek, holding her tight for a moment.

"What's up?" asked Alison.

"Tell her," Abby said to Jules.

And Jules did. Alison was dancing on air the rest of the day.

The time before their departure seemed to fly, both for those leaving and for those staying behind. Jules called George and Bruno and Frank, her mainstays, into the office to break the news. They took it as well as could be expected of hardened men who had dealt with everything life could throw at them over the last decade or so.

George was shocked. Bruno tried to argue, something he'd never done at any time, even when Jules presented some rather, in his opinion, far-fetched ideas. Frank remained his usual imperturbable self, but Jules could've sworn his eyes looked a little watery.

"I've made up my mind," she told them. "It's time. I did this for Mario, and he's gone, and now it's time for me to do whatever it is I'm meant to do. George, you're the real head of the family. I know you'll take this enterprise farther than anyone else ever could."

She stood up and shocked them all when she gave each of them a hug. Frank sniffled. Jules was a little teary too, but she steeled herself for the biggest hurdle: telling Rosa.

"No!" stated Rosa. "No, no, no! You cannot go away and take the little bambinas! No!" She stood there, tapping a wooden spoon against her hand; Jules was half afraid that the older woman intended to use it on her, and it wouldn't have surprised her a bit.

"But, Rosa - " Jules began.

"No! I will not listen to such nonsense. What would Mario say to this?"

Jules was silent for a moment. And then, "I dreamed about Mario last night, after I made up my mind."

"You did?" asked Rosa, hastily crossing herself and sitting down across the table from Jules. "What did he say about this foolishness?"

"He didn't say anything," Jules told her, "just smiled at me and waved."

Rosa pondered this information. She was quiet for so long that Jules thought maybe she'd been forgotten, and she started to rise, to make a quick exit.

"Sit!" said Rosa. "There is only one explanation for this. You will go, and I must go with you."

Jules' eyes grew wide. "But, Rosa, you hate the country!"

"Yes, but I hate you leaving more. And the babies. And there is a house, yes? A cabin? No cave this time?"

"Well, yes. A cabin. I guess it's still standing. But it's a long walk, Rosa. The choppers have very little fuel, and we'll be carrying everything and - "

"Ah, so you think I am too old for this new adventure? If you can walk, just weeks after having the babies, I can walk too."

"But what about Jeanine?" asked Jules, wondering just what she was getting herself into.

"Ah, my sister, she can stay and cook for the men. Yes, I will miss her, but it's not so far that I'll never see her again. She would never leave St. Louis.

"It is settled, then. I will go with you and help you with the little ones."

And so it was.

***

He closed the last notebook and set it carefully on the stack with the others. His story was nearly finished, but there was no real ending. Not yet. No matter how it turned out, he had to make his own ending, and he was ready.

Spring was nearly here; the weather had been mild for days. It was time to leave the mountains and go back east. Time to go home.

He awoke just before dawn, already packed. He stepped through the door one last time, and paused. He would have liked to have taken his notebooks, his story, but no. It would be too much to carry. And anyway, he knew the story by heart.

Maybe someday someone would come across this little cabin and read the words he'd written. Maybe.

He hiked down the mountain and walked along a clear stream that meandered across the valley floor for some miles. Up again, and through Wolf Creek Pass, snow still spotting the landscape. He paused at the halfway mark, looking west for a brief moment.

He continued down the mountain, heading east.

David was going home.

Chapter Thirty-Three

They left St. Louis early one morning in June. As they reached the western edge of the newly settled areas, near Gravois, a solitary figure appeared in the road. Elizabeth ran to him. It was Charles.

Abby and Alison exchanged looks. What could they say?

It took them five days to reach Walt's old cabin. The door was hanging from the hinges, and the place smelled musty. Storm wafted bundles of burning sage throughout, which helped, but it still needed quite a lot of work before it was livable.

They pitched canvas shelters behind the cabin, near the tree line, and went to work. Brad went out to the barn, an old structure with a stone foundation, and found it to be in surprisingly good condition. Inside, he discovered several barrels and rolled them out to the campsite. With Charles' help, he rigged a water filtration system with supplies brought from the city.

EJ and Elizabeth found the old privy near the barn and pronounced it "acceptable," even though they both decided that it was really creepy but not very smelly at all. And it was better than nothing. Abby, Alison, and Emmy searched for rocks and constructed a large firepit. Jules built the fire, and Rosa was ready to take on her cooking duties.

Over supper that night, they sketched out, figuratively, a plan for the homestead and divvied up the workload. Jules, they agreed, should stay nearby with the babies and help Rosa. They couldn't say outright that the old woman needed help, and they certainly wouldn't risk Jules' temper by suggesting that she still needed some recovery time after the birth of the twins. Jules herself did not agree, but she didn't argue either.

Within a month, the garden had been cleared and planted, the cabin repaired, and Brad and Charles were busy building a smokehouse. Abby and Emmy had taken on most of the hunting for the group and spent days at a time in the woods.

Taking a break one day, Emmy leaned back in the grass along the creek and gazed up at the clouds. She let out a heavy sigh and turned on her side to look at Abby.

"Hey, are you awake?"

"Of course. Just thinking."

"Me too. Remember when the bombs hit the infirmary?"

"Not likely to forget that, ever," said Abby, raising up on her elbow. "Why?"

"I know I told you that when they took me, they also took Pops. He looked really bad, Abby, but he lived. He was the one who told me you were dead and tried to get me to . . . well, it doesn't matter. I was just wondering whatever happened to him."

"Why on earth would you waste a single thought on that bastard?" asked Abby, incredulously.

"Oh, not many thoughts," Emmy assured her. "I was hoping he was dead. Because if he's not, I'd like to find him and take care of it myself. But I guess we'll never know. He walked out of my room in St. Louis that day and I never saw him again, not there, not in DC, and not in Chicago."

Abby took a deep breath. "He was my father, Emmy. And he's dead. I promise."

"What? What did you say?"

"You heard me. My father. Pops. And he's dead. I shot him myself."

Emmy was quiet for a moment. "Good."

And they walked back to the cabin, arm in arm.

***

Two days later, as Charles was hauling water from the creek, he heard a noise in the brush. He set down the buckets and drew his gun. He took two steps backwards as he peered into the woods beyond the creek, trying to figure out what was out there. Or who.

Suddenly, he felt cold steel in his spine.

"Who the hell are you?" asked a low voice. "And what are all of you doing here?"

Taken completely by surprise, Charles couldn't speak for a moment as he slowly lowered his gun, dropping it at his feet. And then a voice called out to him.

"Charles, where are you? Rosa's waiting for water to give the babies their bath." It was Elizabeth.

He wondered at his chances of getting the jump on this guy, armed or not, and received the answer as the barrel jabbed him again. He silently willed Elizabeth to turn back. That didn't work either, and she stepped out of the trees and onto the creek bank. Too late.

"David?" she said incredulously. "David?"

He was home.

In a matter of days, he felt as though he'd never left. He told them about all of his travels, his last winter in the cabin, the things he'd seen and done. And he and Abby spent some time together while she filled him in on St. Louis and Chicago and everything in between. She told him about Elizabeth, and Charles, and Mario. And Emmy.

And there was Jules.

It was a hot, dry summer that year. They kept buckets of water near the fire at all times and took their meals outside. They couldn't work very long in the midday sun and so got in the habit of rising well before dawn, working until it became unbearable, and resting throughout the hottest part of the day. Still, the heat was taking a toll, especially on Alison.

She was cranky and snapped at everyone. Then she went into long periods of silence, brooding. She was jumpy, and at least once, Abby heard her throwing up in the bushes behind the barn.

Finally, Storm came to Abby. "You must speak with Alison," she said. "I'm afraid she is just going to make things worse, if she continues like this."

"Make things worse how?" grumbled Abby, still smarting from a comment Alison had tossed in her direction earlier that day during one of her all-too-common tirades.

"That is not my place to say," said Storm. "But you must talk to her, now, today."

"Fine," Abby snapped, then immediately apologized to Storm. Alison had them all on edge, and yes, Abby supposed, it was up to her to put an end to it. She marched off to find Alison.

It didn't take long. Alison was huddled under a tree at the edge of the clearing they had been working on for the last week. She was crying.

Abby sighed. Now she wouldn't get to release some of her frustration by yelling. She sat down beside her old friend and waited. At last, Alison stopped sniffling and turned to Abby.

"Did you come out here to shoot me or just slap me?"

"Neither, actually, but there have definitely been times that the slapping has sounded rather appealing."

"Ha! I'll bet."

The silence grew.

"Ali, what's wrong with you? Are you sick? Storm is worried about something, but she wouldn't tell me. She said to talk to you."

Alison put her head down and mumbled something.

"What?" asked Abby. "For heaven's sake, how bad can it be? You're not dying, are you?"

"May as well be. This is a joke. A sick joke," Alison moaned. "I'm pregnant."

"What?" This time Abby nearly shouted the word. "At your age? I mean, our age? What?"

"I told you," Alison said, "it's a joke, it can't be real! I'm a grandmother, for Pete's sake!"

Abby burst out laughing.

"Oh, sure, you can laugh at me—my daughter is twenty years old and has two adorable babies of her own, and here I am, old and pregnant. Oh, my God."

Abby had managed to stop laughing, but at the look on Alison's face, she couldn't help it. "Well, um, congratulations?"

Alison glared at her. She was doing a lot of that these days.

"Okay, so what did Brad say?"

"Brad? Oh, him. I haven't told him."

"Why the heck not? He'll be tickled to death!" Abby thought of that long-ago day when Zoe and the baby had died.

233

Brad had been crushed; he'd taken off to who knows where and was gone for weeks in the middle of winter.

"He will? I mean, he's been so involved with the girls, but I just figured it was grandpa stuff. You know, play with them, spoil them, then hand them over to Jules."

"Come on, Ali, that's not fair. He changes their diapers and spends hours making toys for them. He loves it—and he'll be thrilled to be a daddy."

Alison still looked doubtful. "Fine, I'll tell him. And I bet he laughs too. It's not funny, it's not a good time, and it's— Oh, shut up already!"

Abby was laughing again. But more than that, she was thanking her lucky stars that it wasn't her in this predicament. "I'm sorry," she said. "I'm just laughing in relief that it's not me, 'cause I'm way too old for that.

"But seriously, Brad will be very, very happy about this. Once . . . once he was almost a father."

Alison sobered up immediately. "I remember. You told me about her. About them. All right. I'll go find him and tell him. Before I lose my nerve.

"Hey, wait a minute! What did you say about being too old?"

Abby jumped up and ran off when Alison swung at her, knowing full well they were almost exactly the same age. And she was laughing again.

Chapter Thirty-Four

Abby closed her eyes and dumped the cup of water on her head. Damn, it was hot already and just the beginning of April. Their first summer here had been brutal, but they'd gotten used to it. Just four years later, and a little heat went a long way; she couldn't handle it like she used to. She shaded her eyes and looked up at the sky. Watching was a hard habit to break, but this time it wasn't prompted by fear of choppers. She was merely checking the weather.

EJ came striding around the corner, her lanky teenage figure making small work of the few yards to the garden, where Abby was working. Her face was etched with concern.

"Mom, really, you shouldn't be out in this heat."

"EJ, for heaven's sake, it's past seven; the sun's going down. I'm fine. I may be old, but I'm far from having heatstroke and that much farther from dropping dead." Abby smiled and tweaked her daughter's braid.

"Nevertheless." EJ tried to assume a more adult demeanor, and almost, but not quite, managed to appear very stern. "It must still be over 80 degrees out here, and you need to rest. I don't have time to be taking care of you too. It's enough with Elizabeth's baby all colicky, and all the kids with heat rash to boot."

Abby sighed. Sometimes this daughter of hers was a trial, but they never would have made it this far if it weren't for EJ. All that reading when she was younger, combined with her father's talent and love for healing, and she had become a very competent doctor herself. All the members of their extended family had made use of her skills at one time or another; yes, even Abby. And Storm was a wonderful teacher.

The two walked companionably into the main house. The original cabin had been slightly enlarged and divided into four rooms: the main room, where they all gathered for meals and meetings; the kitchen; a storage room; and the armory. A cleverly hidden trapdoor opened from the latter room, stairs descending into a bunker. So far, its only use had been for practice drills.

Alison was on KP duty for the evening, and she directed her granddaughters, two adorable miniature sous chefs, in the art of cooking. Alison, who could barely boil water when she'd first appeared, turned out to be quite in demand as a cook. She claimed it all had to do with the amount of tequila she used, but no one paid any attention to that. They all knew that, should tequila once again make an appearance, Alison was not going to be wasting that on a stew.

"Here," she said to Abby. "Take Zoe and keep her entertained. I can't get anything done without at least one hand." Abby sat down and pulled the tiny three-year-old onto her lap. Zoe had been quite a surprise for Alison and Brad, but sometimes things just don't go as planned. They all should have known that by now.

Zoe's presence was a neverending source of amusement for Abby, who often thought smugly that she would never have ended up in this particular predicament. Then she'd stop and remember that certain things had to actually happen before one could have another child, and that wasn't in the picture. Not a few years ago, not now. Nope. And anyway, it was far too late for her.

She snickered aloud. That's what Alison had thought too.

Alison glared at her. It was a pretty common occurrence.

Abby took the little girl into the front room, where it was a bit cooler, and sat down in the old rocker. She could almost fall asleep, but it was just too hot. Besides, she was busy making a mental list of all they had yet to do around the homestead this summer and into the fall.

Jules came in the front door and blew Abby a kiss as she went first into the armory, then into the kitchen. Abby could hear raised voices as the two little girls greeted their mother, and then all three came out to set the table.

The shadows grew longer as the sun dipped low, and still the others had yet to return.

Alison began to look nervously out the window. Abby paced. Jules sat calmly in the corner, cleaning her guns, and EJ entertained the little girls with stories about the animals that lived in the woods.

Things had been quiet for too long.

Over the years, their collective focus had changed from running and hiding to becoming predators themselves, taking a stand, making things happen. For the last four years, living here at Walt's old place, they'd been casual, complacent; trying to put aside old memories and take care of their own, their family.

And then, out of the darkness, came the familiar call. They were back. Abby smiled in relief as Emmy came in with the men. She often became slightly anxious when Emmy wasn't there; she knew she didn't have the strength to lose her again.

Everyone sat down, dinner was served, and conversational bits clashed and collided across the table as David explained the delay.

"Seems that Brad decided Charles here needed a bath, and tried to toss him into the river. By the time we scraped Brad off the ground, old man that he is -" David ducked a biscuit aimed for his head and continued, unabashedly, "we all needed a bath. Could you pass the stew, please?"

"That's it?" asked Alison. "A scuffle among you boys and you're this late and worry us all to death?" She was practically shouting.

"I wasn't worried," said Jules mildly. "Figures."

Her mother spared her a withering glance. "Compulsive gun cleaning? Not worried? Whatever."

Jules shrugged and winked at David. She'd get more details later so she could give Brad a hard time tomorrow. Now wasn't the time, with her mother upset. Alison went back to the kitchen while the others finished dinner.

***

Throughout the summer, the family alternated between working outside, well into the evening to avoid the hottest part of the day, and underground, beneath the main cabin. Charles and David worked to expand and shore up the rooms within the network of caves they'd discovered, while Brad dug out a secondary well that would be accessible only from below.

The "womenfolk," as Charles remarked once—but only once, and he immediately apologized profusely and at length after EJ swept his legs out from under him and unceremoniously pinned him to the ground—worked tirelessly at harvesting, canning, preserving, and gathering. And hunting. Emmy and Abby spent many afternoons tromping through the woods, ever watchful.

Jules took over the scouting. It gave her the creeps to spend so much time inside and below ground; no sky, no trees. Besides, she was good at what she did, and they hadn't had any trouble since they'd come here. It was merely a formality now, a habit.

Robin Tidwell

Chapter Thirty-Five

It was August and hot, a statement that in Missouri was a given and so, therefore, pointless to even remark upon. However, it was also a comment that could be heard often and loudly, even back in the days of electricity and air conditioning.

They'd taken the children down to the river in hopes of cooling off, but the slow-moving current and tepid water did little to provide relief. Everyone lounged in the shade, fanning themselves, speaking desultorily of gardening and needed repairs and other mundane things that kept them all busy, all the time.

Abby stretched and yawned. Several others appeared to be dozing, or close to it, and Abby glanced at Emmy, playing tea party with Rosie and Millie on a blanket. She stood up.

"I have something to tell you all."

EJ looked at her mother in surprise, and Alison frowned. Emmy smiled and nodded encouragement. The others merely roused themselves and looked curious.

"Emmy and I are leaving."

A chorus of voices broke out:

"What?"

"Why?"

"Where are you going?"

Abby held up a hand. "Let me explain, and then we'll answer all your questions." She smiled. "I promise, we'll keep you in the loop, and we're not going far."

The conversation became animated, heated at times, and then Brad intervened.

"Abby's right. This is what they need to do. More important, it's what they want. And after everything that's happened over the years, I think we all just need to shut up about it. Like she said, it's not far. We can visit; they can visit.

"They've more than done their part over the years, and it's time both of them get a say in what they want. Now, let's figure out the best time and the most optimal way of doing this. Got it?"

There was a bit more grumbling, and EJ looked troubled.

"What's wrong, EJ?" asked her mother, sitting back down.

"Um, well . . . am I supposed to go with you?" EJ frowned. "It's not that I don't want to, exactly, but . . ."

Abby laughed. "EJ, you more than qualify as an adult now, able to make your own decisions, even if you aren't quite what we used to call 'legal.' After everything you've done and been put through, you're all grown up now. I'd love to have you come with us, but it's your call. I promise I won't be mad either way."

"Really, Mom? Then I can stay? I still have so much to learn from Storm, and well, you know, she's pretty old now. I mean, so are you, but - "

"Emmaline! I am nowhere near her age. Fifty isn't old!"

"Gee, Mom, you haven't called me that in, like, ever. Or never. And you're a little past fifty, anyway."

"Fine," said Abby. "In my fifties; is that better?" She sounded grumpy, but EJ could see the smile Abby was trying to hide. "And still not old."

"Okay, okay. I get it. But I can still stay, right?"

"Yes, daughter of mine. You can stay." Abby hugged EJ, held her tight, then let her go. She'd be fine. They'd both be fine.

The next week was spent in dividing up supplies and tools and packing as much as could be carried. Brad volunteered to make the trip with them, but he wasn't staying. Alison and Zoe were here, after all. He still couldn't believe he was a father after all these years.

Jules wanted to go too, of course, at least to help them get settled in, but Abby told her no. The two of them took a long walk together the day before departure.

"Come on, Abby, let me go with you, at least for a few days or so."

"No, honey. You've got responsibilities right here, those two gorgeous girls. Besides, the rest of them couldn't do without you either."

"Sure they could," Jules argued. "Mom'll be here, and David, and it's just for a few days."

"No," Abby told her again. "It's enough that Brad's going with us . . ."

And then Jules understood.

***

Everyone turned out to see them off. Abby was tempted to walk backwards, just to keep them all in sight a bit longer: Jules and her daughters, David, Elizabeth, Charles, Storm, Zoe. EJ, who'd nearly changed her mind at the last minute, but kept her eyes dry and promised to visit soon. She stood there with Storm, waving, blowing kisses. And Alison. Dear Ali had saved her butt on more than one occasion, and fate had thrown them into some interesting situations.

Abby looked at Emmy, smiling and by her side, and waved one last time, resolutely setting her face to the future . . . and then began walking back in time.

***

The three of them reached the top of Purple Mountain in the late afternoon as the sun lit up the meadow below. The old campsite was horribly overgrown, but still recognizable. They had, after all, spent a long winter up here. Brad walked over to the graves, barely discernible in the brush. He gazed down at them for a long time, remembering his wife and all the others who had died there.

They hiked through the trees, down to site 4. The paths had disappeared completely. Reaching the bottom, the gravel road peeking out from the tall weeds, they walked through the old camp, barely glancing at the pile of rubble that marked the old infirmary where Emmy had once died, and Riley had been born.

They crossed the creek, the sturdy old bridge still usable, and passed the leaning office buildings with gaping holes in roofs and walls. Up the hill, to the cave.

They were home. Full circle. Where it had begun, so it would end.

Brad returned to Walt's place, to Alison and Zoe, to Jules and the others. He had much to look forward to, and he never looked back again. It was enough.

Abby and Emmy settled into the old cave. They spent the next months preparing for winter, laying in a supply of firewood, hunting and fishing, and growing a small, late garden down in the meadow. They hiked and explored and talked long into the evenings, making up for those lost years and those that came after, trying to survive.

Content in each other's company, they were satisfied that this place, right here, was where they were meant to be. As it always was.

Winter came, and the rain and the storms.

Robin Tidwell

Epilogue

The dark clouds came from the west, boiling and black. The wind whipped across the land, shoving aside everything in its path, everything that wasn't secure. The man behind that wind, responsible for the coming storm, figuratively, if not literally, was safely ensconced behind his walls as he watched the clouds move east.

Unbreachable walls, impenetrable, and this time he would succeed. He laughed wryly at his own wit, comparing himself to every supervillain, fictional or otherwise, because he knew without a doubt that he was the best. Indeed, he was the only one of the original plotters still alive, thanks to his planning and foresight and, of course, his intelligence. And VADER. Credit where credit is due, he supposed.

He shrugged. Too bad, really, that so many had died. Yes. Terrible. But it had made his plans so much easier to execute. And now, when they all least expected it, there was one more move to make.

Just one.

Repeat.

ABOUT THE AUTHOR

Born in St. Louis, Missouri, Robin graduated from Parkway Central at the end of her junior year and went on to college . . . five times. Nearly 30 years later, on a whim, she looked over her transcripts and re-enrolled, completing not quite sixty hours of credit in just over one calendar year. Her degree, from Columbia College, is a combined major of psychology, sociology, and criminal justice.

Robin's writing career began at the age of eight, when her grandmother insisted she read Gone With the Wind before taking her to see the movie. Inspired by Margaret Mitchell, she began scribbling little booklets of stories, and was the editor of her elementary school newspaper and a columnist in high school. She submitted a short story to Seventeen magazine and was promptly rejected, but still keeps a copy of the manuscript in her desk.

Robin has worked as a snack bar cook, a salad prepper, a camp counselor, a waitress, a receptionist, a housekeeper, a freelancer, an editor, and an employment consultant and manager. She's also been in car sales, skin care sales, cookware sales, advertising sales, and MLM. She's owned and operated an entrepreneurial conglomerate, a cleaning service, an old-time photography studio, a bookstore, and a publishing house.

Six years ago, Robin and her husband Dennis moved back to St. Louis after many years in Columbia, Sedalia, Colorado Springs, Durango, and Granbury and Tolar, Texas. They live with their youngest son, a dog, a cat, and a puppy.

Robin Tidwell

REDUCED

A devastating biological agent is about to be released, to be tested in remote areas. Rumor has it, though, that there is more to this than meets the eye. One group makes plans to hide out, and survive, in case that rumor proves to be truth. Meeting at an abandoned summer camp near St. Louis, Missouri, a dozen old friends gather after the alarm is raised.

Life becomes more precious, more tenuous, as time passes. Government controls tighten, people are herded into the city—or killed. Towns are obliterated. And soon, the enemy agenda becomes obvious.

Abby will come face-to-face with death, bear the responsibility for a young girl, and endure the severing of childhood relationships in the most terrible way imaginable.

From mere concealment to reconnaissance to aiding a rebellion, where will it end? Will the entire region be decimated, and who will be left alive to know?

REUSED

Colonel Barton has been replaced, and the new commander is sending his henchman, Major Blake, to scour the outlying areas and remove any insurgents. Abby and the girls have remained in the cave at the camp, relatively safe for now, but plans are underway to eliminate all of them . . . for personal reasons, known only to the commander himself.

Soon, however, worlds will collide as Captain Alison Hinson is transferred in from Chicago. In spite of her background, Alison is horrified by the tactics of her superiors in the field and begins to question her own stance on the new government. As she puts together the pieces of the past, she realizes that she and Abby are kindred spirits, faced with a mission not of their own choosing, but of circumstance.

Across the country, while officials and mercenaries live the high life, the citizenry are faced with more sanctions, more regulation, and fewer necessities. Pockets of rebellion are quickly quelled, but incidents continue to increase as more people make the decision to go underground. Literally.

From abandoned caves below St. Louis itself to a subterranean river winding north into Illinois, REUSED will tell you more, perhaps, than you truly wish to know about the potential for the utter collapse of our civilization.

INTERVIEW WITH ABBY

Good morning, Abby. I have to tell you, this is kind of strange—interviewing the main character in my novel, REDUCED.

Yeah . . . imagine how I feel . . . I'm not real comfortable with all this publicity.

Well, let's start with you. Tell us a little about yourself.

Not much to tell, really. My parents died when I was eight, I went to live with Aunt Lois. She was okay. Not a lot of fun for a kid to be around. I kept going to camp every summer; she was happy to get rid of me for a few weeks and I met a lot of great friends there.

Where did you go to college?

Oh, a small school, in central Missouri. Not much to tell about that either. I finished my degree and got out of there as soon as I could.

And then?

Then I bummed around Arizona and New Mexico for a while; sometimes up into Colorado. Did a few odd jobs to get by, worked on a couple ranches.

How did you learn about tracking and hunting, and all those other skills you show us in REDUCED?

Some of those I actually learned about at camp. But the rest, well, I met this old Indian out west, his name was Peytah. He taught me all about animal habits, tracks, hiding out. All that stuff. Came in handy, wouldn't you say?

Well, yes, absolutely! How do you feel about your role in REDUCED?

Honestly, I was kind of surprised. I usually like to stay in the background, taking care of things, behind the scenes, you know? So here I find myself front and center, and it was a little uncomfortable. But then, well, everything changed. When the world as you know it has so completely vanished, you do what you gotta do I guess.

Tell us about Juliet.

Oh, Jules. She can be so sweet, but she's really a tough kid. Even when she first came to us, she was so small but so determined. She'd just lost her parents—I don't even want to know the details of that, and she's never talked about it—and she really just took to me. Not sure why, except I was the one who found her that day. Maybe I reminded her of her mom, I don't know. But she was eager to learn, and very responsible. She doesn't seem to have any real issues, growing up like she did, which is kind of surprising; on the other hand, it's all she's known.

So what's next for you two?

It's been pretty quiet around here for a few years; five or six, actually. I'm sure things are going to pick up, I've seen a lot of activity in the sky lately. We never stop watching and waiting. Colonel Barton couldn't possibly give up so easily, and Co-opCom never stops—we do hear things out here. But, at the same time, we just carry on. Until the next . . . whatever it is that's coming. Because it'll show up—"they" will show up, here, sometime. Soon.

INTERVIEW WITH JULIET

Hello, Juliet. How are things going these days?

About the same as usual, why? I mean, not a lot happening, really, but I have a feeling it's going to get busy pretty soon.

Well, I actually meant that as a general question, but as long as we're talking about what's going to happen, what exactly do you mean?

I dunno for sure, but Abby seems a little on edge lately and well, it's been awhile since anyone has bothered us. But we've both seen those choppers up north.

I see. So what do you think about living out there in the woods, watching and waiting all the time? Does it bother you at all?

Nope. Been that way for a long time now, let's see, since I was nine. I mean, it's just been the three of us since then but Abby and I were out here a long time before that too. With the others. Besides, I like the woods. It's quiet, it's peaceful. So far.

You were barely four years old when Abby found you; you'd just lost your parents. How long were you alone before she brought you back to the camp?

Couple days, I guess. I don't remember much of that, and I'd rather not talk about it, if you don't mind. A lot has happened since then and I guess I've had to grow up pretty quickly. Far as I'm concerned, my life started when Abby showed up; but she thinks I need to remember my

mom and dad too, so I do try to remember before . . . you know, before VADER.

Tell me about life in the camp, when everyone was there.

Well, you know, we did a lot of stuff. Abby went off on scouting trips a lot so I stayed with Emmy then . . . well, at least after Grammy . . . you know. And everyone helped teach me, like my schooling and all. Pops was so great at math, he really had patience with me. And I learned to shoot, and to hide in the woods. And tracking. That part was fun, really! And Ted was a great cook—I'm learning more about that now, but I'd rather be out in the woods somewhere. Abby says I have to learn everything, just in case she . . . just in case.

And then later? What's it been like these last few years?

More of the same, really. We check out the perimeter pretty regularly, and watch the skies a lot. We keep things simple, and try to stay under the radar. And EJ keeps us pretty busy, what with all her questions. Wow, never knew someone could talk so much! But she's learning stuff, too—she's a lot better than I am at starting a fire, but not so good at hitting the target when we practice. She's still pretty little though. And I help with her school lessons too, she's really smart, even at math!

EJ?

Um, yeah, guess I'm not really supposed to talk about her. Abby'd have a fit, probably. But after you've read the book, you'll know about her.

Well, since I WROTE the book . . .

Oh, right. Well, you know what I mean! Geez, Abby's always after me to be more specific, say what I mean, blah, blah, blah. I meant your readers, duh! So, yeah, after they finish the book, they'll know about EJ. Better?

Yes, thanks. And Abby's right, you know.

Oh sure, take her side! Wait a minute . . . yeah, I know what you're gonna say. Never mind.

You're probably right, Juliet. So, can we talk more after REUSED comes out in December?

Yeah, sure. Okay. I can probably do that. Not like my schedule's all booked up or anything. Well, probably. Guess you'd know that better than I . . .

www.ingramcontent.com/pod-product-compliance
Lightning Source LLC
Chambersburg PA
CBHW050022180626
46810CB00002B/538